S0-AJW-343

The HARDY BOYS *Mystery Stories*
BY FRANKLIN W. DIXON

"AFTER HIM!" CRIED JOE.

THE
SINISTER
SIGN POST

BY

FRANKLIN W. DIXON

NEW YORK
GROSSET & DUNLAP
Publishers

Printed in the United States of America

CONTENTS

CHAPTER I

THE MISSING RACE-HORSE

"I'M glad there is peace and quiet in the air this morning," said Mrs. Hardy, stirring her coffee. "I really believe this is the first breakfast we've had together in weeks without a mystery of some kind to digest along with ham and eggs."

Frank Hardy, who was reading part of the morning paper, looked up.

"No mystery?" he exclaimed. "What of the football game this afternoon, Mother? Isn't it a mystery whether or not Bayport High will win?"

Joe Hardy, a year younger than his brother, looked up from another section of the news sheet.

"And there's a first-class mystery about the ability of that marvelous new horse, *Topnotch*. He's going to race at Spurtown track tomorrow. Some say he can't be beaten, but nobody knows for sure."

Fenton Hardy, their father, who was reading his mail, looked up a moment. "I've seen *Topnotch* run in the South, and he certainly is a remarkable horse," he said.

Then he turned to his letters, and tore open an envelope. The famous detective smiled at his wife.

"There is still another mystery, as I see from this note," he said. "Are certain foreigners, plotting against our government, secretly buying munitions and hiding them in this country? If so, where are they concealing them? That's what I should call a Number One, Class A mystery."

Aunt Gertrude, who had been fussing about in the kitchen, poked her head in the doorway and peered at them over her spectacles.

"And it's another mystery how those two boys can dawdle so long over their breakfast when I'm waiting to give them some work," she snapped.

"I give up," laughed Mrs. Hardy. "I merely have to mention the word mystery to be overwhelmed with several of them. That's what comes of living in a family of detectives."

Mr. Hardy had been connected at one time with the New York City Police Department, but had later organized his own private detective agency. So successful had he been that he was now internationally famous, and recognized as one of the most brilliant men in his profession in the country.

Frank and Joe, his sons, had inherited much of his ability, and had succeeded in solving many puzzling mysteries independently. It was only natural, therefore, that mention of the word "mystery" in the Hardy household should have brought such a ready response from everyone.

The two boys left the table and went out into the hall to telephone to their chum, Chet Morton, who was to play for Bayport High in the football game at Seneca that afternoon.

"How are you feeling, big fella?" asked Frank, when his friend answered the phone.

"Couldn't be better. How is Joe?"

"His arm is still out of commission. He'll be just a spectator today."

"Tough luck."

Joe Hardy had injured himself in a game the previous Saturday, and, much to his disgust, the doctor had ordered him to play no more the rest of the season.

"It will be up to you and Tony Printo to bring home the bacon," said Frank. "We'll be rooting for you, Chet."

"We'll miss Joe against that Seneca outfit. You're driving over, I suppose?"

"Yes, we'll go in the roadster. Good luck, Chet."

"So long."

The boys spent the rest of the morning washing the car. Shortly after lunch they set out for Seneca, which was the goal of all Bayport football fans that day. The local High School and Seneca Tech were old football rivals, and their annual gridiron struggle was a county classic. The loss of Joe Hardy, star halfback of the Bayport eleven, was a serious blow, for their opponents had an unusually strong team.

"Makes me furious I can't play," grumbled the younger brother as the two drove along.

Fifteen miles out of Bayport the roadster suddenly came to a stop.

"Now what's wrong?" said Frank. "I thought we checked everything."

He got out, raised the hood, and explored the car's interior. After twenty minutes of fuming and fussing he discovered the trouble.

The gas tank was empty!

"I thought you bought gasoline yesterday," said Frank to his brother.

"I thought *you* did."

Car after car had been passing them on the way to the football game. Now, when they wanted help, there wasn't any in sight. A truck finally came along but the driver refused to stop. A big passenger auto also sped by. Another ten minutes flew along before a friendly motorist drew up and agreed to tow them to the nearest gas station.

"Going to the game?" asked the attendant, as he filled up the tank.

"What's left of it," said Joe. "I expect we'll be late."

"Why don't you take the short cut through Kempton?" the man suggested, indicating a side road. "It will get you over to Seneca in twenty minutes. Don't take the turn to the left about three miles down, though, for that leads across to Spurtown."

The Hardy boys thanked him and set off down the side road, but after a few minutes' travel they were wishing they had taken the longer route. Recent rains had left the highway in bad shape. To add to their grief, a rear tire blew out with a dismal bang, and they lost further time replacing it with the spare.

"What a trip!" groaned Frank, toiling with the wrench.

A big box truck just then lumbered down the road and drew to a stop abreast of them. A colored man in the driver's seat leaned out.

"Kin you gemmen tell me which is de right way to Spurtown?" he drawled.

"Straight ahead and first turn to your left," Frank told him.

The man touched his cap.

"Thank you, suh," he said, and drove on.

As the vehicle disappeared over the brow of a hill, the Hardy boys noticed that it had Kentucky license plates.

"That truck is from Old Kentucky, eh?" said Joe. "It wouldn't take much guessing to tell what's inside."

"Race-horse," replied Frank promptly. "That fellow is on his way to the Spurtown track. The races open tomorrow."

"Let's go."

"We'd better get to that football game first. Time enough to think about the races afterward."

Suddenly, in the distance, they heard a sharp report that sounded like a pistol shot. It appeared to come from some point at the right of the road a short distance ahead.

"Shooting?" said Joe.

"Sounded like it. Perhaps that truck turned to the right instead of the left, and something happened to it."

The boys climbed into their car and drove on. After a ride of a quarter of a mile they reached a crossroad. One branch led to the left, with a sign post proclaiming, "Spurtown, 3 Miles;" the other wound off toward a wooded section to the right.

There was no sign of the truck. The boys

agreed that they had no time to spend investigating the mysterious shot, so they sped on without further delay toward Seneca.

They got there just in time for the opening kick-off, and were soon raising their share of the bedlam created by the Bayport High rooting section as Chet Morton and his cohorts went into action.

"Please," said a guttural voice at Frank's elbow, "vould you be so good as to oxplain dis game to me? I do not onnerstand."

Frank looked up. A swarthy, well-dressed stranger was raising his hat politely.

"Well, you see, sir, it's this way—Yeah, Bayport!" the Hardy boy roared exultantly as Chet Morton caught a forward pass and raced down the field to be tackled on Seneca's twenty-yard line. "Oh, boy, did you see that?" For a moment the man at his side was forgotten while Frank joined in the Bayport yell.

"It is permit to t'row de ball?" inquired the stranger.

The lad tried to explain the game to the man, but the foreigner, who introduced himself as a Mr. Vilnoff, and who said he was living near Bayport, became more and more muddled. He plied Frank with countless questions, and when the first half was called, with Bayport leading 13 to 7, the boy was heartily sick of the task of introducing the stranger to the mysteries of American football. It was spoiling his own enjoyment of the game, and he was quite sure Vilnoff was not gaining anything from the explanations. During intermission Frank tried to lose his interrogator in the crowd, but when the third quarter began the swarthy gentleman popped up beside him.

"Now tell me if you vould be so good," he resumed, "why is it dat man always blows his vistle?" as a Seneca player was thrown for a loss.

Patiently Frank attempted to explain the reason for this, but the middle of an ~xciting gridiron struggle is no time to attempt to give a lesson in football. Vilnoff made himself a nuisance throughout the game. The only redeeming feature of the afternoon, as far as Frank was concerned, was the fact that Bayport High marched off the field victorious. At that, he had to tell Vilnoff the name of the winning team.

"It was so good of you. I am afraid I have been very stupid," apologized the man. "You go to Bayport High School, yes?"

"I'm a senior," admitted Frank.

"I once knew one of your teachers, Monsieur Carriere."

"Oh, yes. He teaches French."

"I met him in Europe, at a university," said Vilnoff. "T'ank you so much."

Frank escaped as soon as he could. After visiting Chet and the other members of the victorious team in the dressing room, he joined Joe at the car.

"Have a nice time?" grinned his brother, who had been greatly amused by Frank's plight all afternoon.

"Don't mention it," retorted the lad. "That fellow Vilnoff is a real nuisance."

The next morning, however, he had forgotten all about the too affable Mr. Vilnoff. A message from Chet Morton gave the Hardys other things to think about. He telephoned before the boys sat down to breakfast.

"Listen, Frank," he said excitedly. "I think I've a first-rate mystery for you. Want to hear about it?"

"Shoot."

"You remember reading about *Topnotch,* that valuable race horse that was going to run at Spurtown today?"

"*Was?*"

"It doesn't look as if he'll run! He's disappeared! The owner is just about frantic. *Topnotch* was shipped to Spurtown and should have arrived yesterday. He hasn't reached the track!"

CHAPTER II

THE JOCKEY

"THE horse never arrived?" exclaimed Frank. "Was he sent by train?"

"No, by truck. And even the truck has disappeared," Chet said.

"The driver may have taken the wrong road. It's pretty hard to lose a truck."

"Just the same, the owner of the race-horse believes *Topnotch* didn't disappear by accident. I thought I should call you up and tell you about it, anyhow. You and Joe may get some bright ideas that will help out.

"And here's something else: there was a bad explosion in the munitions factory at Renside last night and the police think foreign agents may have been at the bottom of it. That's another mystery for you."

"We can't do anything about the factory," Frank answered, "but I have a hunch about the horse."

"What is it?"

"Can't tell you just now. I may be all wrong, but Joe and I will go to work on it. Much obliged, Chet."

Frank hung up the receiver and told his brother the news. Joe whistled in surprise.

"So *Topnotch* is missing. Probably stolen. The horse is worth a lot of money. But what's your hunch, Frank?"

"Remember the truck that passed us on the short cut yesterday? The driver was on his way to Spurtown."

"*Topnotch* may have been in that truck, all right," Joe agreed. "It was queer, too, about the shot we thought we heard."

"Won't do any harm to investigate. Let's go to the races at Spurtown this afternoon. We can nose around and make a few inquiries while we're there."

"I'm game."

The moment they mentioned their intention of going to the track, their Aunt Gertrude raised objections.

"Horse-racing, Laura?" she exclaimed in horror to Mrs. Hardy. "Do you mean to tell me you will let those boys go to a horse-race?"

"I can't see anything wrong in it," said Mrs. Hardy mildly.

"Nothing wrong in it!" snorted Aunt Gertrude. "It's sinful, that's all that's wrong with it. Liquor and gambling and horse-racing all go together. Let a boy go to a horse-race and he is on the way to perdition. However, they're your boys, not mine. I wash my hands of the affair. If you think it's all right for them to go in for such a wicked sport as horse-racing, that's your business. But mark my words, Laura, there will come a day when you'll regret it bitterly!"

Aunt Gertrude was in a fine state of righteous indignation. From the recesses of her memory she dug up an anecdote about a promising young man who once went to a horse-race and soon afterwards lost his job and was sent to jail for forging a check.

"And not fifteen years later he died of liver trouble!" concluded Aunt Gertrude triumphantly.

"All from going to a horse-race?" inquired Joe innocently.

"That was the first false step. Up to that day he was as fine a boy as you would wish to see. But he died a ruined and broken man. They had to take up a collection to bury him."

Aunt Gertrude's impressive warnings failed to convince the boys that they should remain quietly at home and read a good book instead of going to Spurtown. After lunch they slipped out of the house and managed to get away in the car before the good lady could deliver another sermon.

The races were being held in connection with the annual Spurtown County Fair, and the grounds presented a gay scene. The music of a merry-go-round, the shouts of barkers, and the crack of rifles in a shooting gallery rose above the dull roar of the crowd. Farmers and their families strolled through the stock buildings and down the midway. The grandstand facing the race-track was already filling up.

"Let's have a frankfurter," Joe suggested.

"Good idea."

They stopped at the nearest refreshment stand. A timid little woman was buying an ice cream cone for her small boy. As the two boys came up to the counter she took a five-dollar bill from a worn purse. The man behind the counter made change briskly.

"Twenty-thirty-forty-fifty-one dollar-two-three-four dollars, and thank you, ma'am," he said rapidly, and turned to Frank and Joe.

"Two dogs?" he asked in a loud voice.

Frank had noticed that a trick had been perpetrated. The man had made change for only four dollars instead of five, pocketing the extra bill himself. The woman, confused, looked at the coins and bills in front of her, began to count them, lost track, and started counting all over again.

"You owe the lady a dollar, I think," said Frank.

The vendor scowled.

"You mind your own business, young fellow,'' he said impudently. ''She got **her** change.''

''We'll check it for you, ma'am,'' said **Joe.** ''Look—one dollar, two-three-three-ninety. One dollar short, and we saw you give him **a** five-dollar bill.''

Frank regarded the fellow with level eyes.

''Come on!'' he said. ''Give the lady the extra dollar.''

''Funny. Guess I must have made a mistake,'' grumbled the vendor, reluctantly handing over the money.

''Perhaps we'd better tell one of the fairgrounds constables to keep an eye on you,'' Joe suggested.

''Thank you ever so much,'' exclaimed the woman. ''I had only five dollars, and if I'd lost a whole dollar it would have meant less food for my family this week. It was mighty kind of you to help me.''

''That's all right,'' they assured her, and drifted off into the crowd, regardless of the vendor's baleful glance.

They made their way to the jockey's quarters underneath the big grandstand, and there made inquiries about the race-horse *Topnotch.*

''No, sirree, that there hawss has plumb dropped clean out of sight,'' drawled a red-faced trainer. ''Somethin' mighty queer about that business.''

"Perhaps the truck is lost," Joe suggested.

"Should have turned up by now," remarked the attendant. "Nope, I think *Topnotch* has done been stolen."

He moved off toward the paddock where several sleek horses were being saddled and put into condition for the opening race.

"There *is* a mystery, then," Frank remarked. "I wonder if it has anything to do with that truck we saw on the road yesterday?"

The boys were on their way to make further inquiries about the missing race-horse when they noticed the small son of the woman they had helped standing on the outskirts of the crowd. He looked so forlorn and friendless that Frank said, "What's the matter, sonny? Not having any fun?"

The lad shook his head. "I haven't any money," was his reply.

"That's tough," returned Frank sympathetically. "I guess we'd better see what we can do about it. You come along with us."

Obediently the youngster walked with the Hardy boys, his eyes brightening. At a nearby booth Frank saw a vendor selling kites of all sizes and descriptions.

"Would you like one?" he asked the little fellow.

The youngster nodded his head energetically,

so Frank promptly bought him a large, brightly-colored kite. Then they adjourned to a nearby field to try it out. There was a stiff breeze blowing, and soon the toy was riding high in the wind. Frank then handed the string to the happy boy. The Hardys left him running joyfully about the field, admiring his new possession, as it soared far above the fair-grounds.

A gloomy looking young man had been sitting on the fence watching them. He was very small, appearing to weigh in the neighborhood of a hundred pounds. He had a sad, oldish face.

"Looks to me like a jockey," remarked Joe as they approached the stranger.

"That kid is sure having a lot of fun," said the young man on the fence, motioning toward the boy with the kite. "More fun than I'm having, anyway," he added, a tinge of bitterness in his voice.

"What's the trouble?" asked Frank.

"I was supposed to ride *Topnotch* today, and now the horse has disappeared and I'm out of luck."

"Are you Jockey Ivan?" asked Frank, who had noticed the name of *Topnotch's* prospective rider in the newspaper.

"That's me. A jockey without a horse."

The Hardy boys were interested. From

Ivan they might learn a few more particulars about the mysterious disappearance of the race-horse.

Their alertness to possibilities was what had made Frank and Joe such successful amateur detectives. A little while before they had proved their abilities in solving a mystery concerning a hidden treasure, as related in "The Tower Treasure." Later adventures, such as those recounted in "The Secret of the Old Mill," "The Shore Road Mystery," "While the Clock Ticked," and other volumes served to confirm the fact. The lads had won a reputation for themselves while still at school, and had earned enough money in rewards to build up substantial bank accounts.

"The Hidden Harbor Mystery," immediately preceding the present volume, describes one of the most baffling cases ever tackled by the Hardy boys. They emerged from it with credit after undergoing numerous thrilling adventures in the neighborhood of an old Southern mansion. Now they seemed to be confronting a new mystery in connection with the South—that of a valuable race-horse.

"Do you think the truck driver can be trusted?" Joe asked the jockey.

"He's as honest as the day is long," returned Ivan promptly. "Both he and the fellow inside the truck are absolutely above board. They have worked for the owner of the horse for years. My own idea is that they've all been kidnaped.''

''Why?'' asked Frank.

Ivan shrugged.

''You're asking me!'' he replied. ''I haven't the slightest idea. The kidnapers can't race the horse on any other track because *Topnotch* is registered, and would be recognized wherever he goes. I can't figure the thing out.''

''Ransom, probably?'' Joe suggested.

''Maybe,'' agreed Ivan. ''In the meantime, the race meet is going on and I haven't a horse to ride. I've been offered a few mounts, of course, but—aw, shucks, after riding *Topnotch* these other nags are like a bunch of mules. So long, fellows, I guess I'll go over and watch the next race.''

Thereupon he jumped down from the fence and sauntered away.

''He seems to be a nice chap,'' said Frank. ''I wish we could help him.''

''If the horse is being held for ransom the owner will hear from the thieves soon enough,'' remarked Joe. ''Let's go over to the track.''

A few minutes later, after the race had been run, Frank spied Mr. Vilnoff, his acquaintance of the previous day. What interested him particularly was the fact that the foreigner was engaged in animated conversation with Jockey

Ivan. Both appeared to be angry, and Vilnoff was gesticulating wildly as he spoke.

"Looks like an argument," chuckled Joe.

Vilnoff and the jockey were standing at the foot of a slope, at the top of which a number of cars were parked. As the Hardy boys watched they saw another machine swing in from the road and edge into the parking space. Its bumper nudged one of the automobiles at the top of the incline. Apparently the brakes of the parked car had not been firmly set, for the slight collision was enough to thrust the front wheels over the brink of the embankment and set them into motion.

Slowly the auto began to head down the slope. It was unoccupied. As it picked up speed the horrified boys saw that it was plunging directly toward Vilnoff and the jockey, who were so absorbed in their argument that they did not notice what was happening.

"They'll be hurt!" yelled Frank. He shouted a warning:

"Ivan! Vilnoff!"

But the pair did not hear him. The car raced on!

CHAPTER III

Joe Hardy was already rushing to the rescue.

Even if Vilnoff and the jockey did realize their peril in time to dodge out of its path, the runaway car would continue its headlong course and crash into the crowd near the track rail, to claim a toll of serious injuries, if not of lives.

Joe leaped across the intervening space, his dash perfectly timed. He jumped onto the running board of the car, wrenched open the door, and reached inside to grab the emergency brake. By this time the automobile was thundering down the slope.

The boy pulled back the brake just in time. The speed of the car slackened, then ground to a full stop not three feet away from Vilnoff and the jockey. They whirled around, alarmed by the screech of metal and the shouts of Frank.

"That was a narrow squeak," Joe said calmly, as he climbed out.

Jockey Ivan, pale and frightened, blurted out, "We'd have been knocked clean out onto the track if you hadn't stopped the car. I didn't even hear the thing coming.''

Vilnoff mopped his brow with a handkerchief.

"A ner-row escape, yes!" he said.

Frank ran up at that moment. ''That was quick work, Joe. It took nerve, too. If that brake had failed——''

Suddenly the situation took a different turn.

"I saw you!" broke in a truculent voice. ''Trying to steal my car, hey? By George, I'm going to turn you over to the police, you young rascal. Not only tried to steal my car, but mighty nearly smashed it up in the bargain.''

The group gazed in astonishment at a stout, angry, red-faced man who had come bustling up to them. He waved a cane in the air.

''You stole my car from the parking space!'' he accused Joe. ''You can't deny it!''

''Don't be silly,'' snapped Frank. ''He did nothing of the kind.''

''He did!'' roared the owner. ''If he hadn't lost control of it he'd have been clear away with it by now.''

Joe was dumbfounded. ''You left your machine at the top of the slope without setting the emergency brake,'' he cried angrily. ''It might have injured a dozen people—maybe killed some of them. You ought to be arrested for negligence.''

''*I* ought to be arrested!'' yelped the fat man,

turning purple with wrath. "*You* ought to be arrested, you young scoundrel."

"Go ahead and try it," invited Frank coolly. "We can dig up half a dozen witnesses who saw my brother jump into the machine and stop it from running through the crowd. Maybe the police will have something to say about the careless way you left your car parked at the top of the hill."

The fat man began to calm down. Finally, muttering to himself, he got into the auto and drove off toward the exit.

When the Hardy boys looked around they found that Vilnoff had disappeared into the crowd. Jockey Ivan, however, had remained. He shook hands gratefully with the boys.

"I guess I owe my life to you," he told Joe shakily. "It was a mighty brave thing for you to do. Not many fellows would have risked it."

"Forget it," grinned the younger Hardy.

"I wonder where Mr. Vilnoff went?" Frank remarked suddenly.

"You know him?" Ivan asked.

"I met him at a football game yesterday. Is he a friend of yours?"

Ivan looked somewhat embarrassed.

"Well—er—yes," he answered very slowly. "That is——"

Then he stopped. It was plain that the jockey did not care to discuss the matter any further, for he edged away without saying anything more about Vilnoff.

During the next hour the Hardy boys watched the races and hung around the paddock, hoping to hear something that might give them a clue in the case of the missing *Topnotch*. Although they heard the affair discussed freely, they learned nothing that might be of any value to them. Most of the track followers were positive that the horse had been stolen.

"It seems odd," remarked Frank, "that the van should have been going toward Spurtown on that particular road. If it had come directly from Kentucky it would have reached Spurtown by the State Highway."

"I guess the driver lost his way."

"Perhaps he was misdirected purposely. I think it might pay us to have another look at the crossroads."

The boys got into their car and drove away from the track, heading toward the route on which they had driven into Seneca the previous afternoon. They had scarcely left Spurtown, however, when a horn sounded sharply behind them. Frank, who was at the wheel, was forced to pull over to permit a big, high-powered car to pass.

The huge automobile was traveling at an excessive rate of speed. As it hurtled by, taking so much of the road that Frank was forced into the ditch, they had a glimpse of a uniformed chauffeur in front and a crouching figure in the rear seat. The big car flashed past and went roaring on its way in a cloud of dust.

"Road-hog!" growled Frank.

"Some of those fellows think they own the earth!" Joe said angrily, as his brother tried to get their own auto back onto the road again.

Fortunately the ditch was shallow and there was no mud. The experience was nevertheless annoying, especially since they had given the other machine plenty of room in which to get by.

"Did you get a good look at that fellow in the back seat, Frank?"

"No, I was too busy trying to keep us from being sideswiped. What about him?"

"I didn't get any more than a glimpse of him, but I have a pretty good notion we've seen him before."

"Where?"

"I may be wrong," said Joe, "but I think the man was Vilnoff."

Frank whistled.

"He seems in a terrific hurry, wherever he's going. Vilnoff must be worth plenty of money, if that's his car. He strikes me as a queer sort of individual."

The big automobile was soon out of sight, and by the time the boys reached the crossroads it was nowhere to be seen.

"We'll work on the theory that the horse van didn't turn toward Spurtown after all," said Frank. "It certainly didn't go on toward Seneca, and we know it couldn't possibly have turned back. So we'll just investigate this abandoned route straight ahead."

Slowly they drove down the side road, looking for tracks of the van. At length, in a sandy part they discovered a tire treadmark evidently made by a heavy truck. They followed it, lost it, and picked it up again until it came to a narrow road that led off to the right. This was a mere trail, muddy in places. Evidently the van had turned in at this point.

Frank and Joe were growing excited. They had high hopes that they might discover the missing truck and horse hidden somewhere along this old road. It was difficult driving, for the trail was rutty and bumpy. The car lurched and swung.

Finally the road petered out altogether. Although they could still make out a clearing ahead in the fading light, they saw that it was nothing but a trail. On a tree nearby they spied a crudely scrawled signboard which read:

"ROAD AHEAD DANGEROUS. DO NOT PASS."

The Hardy boys got out of their car.

"Let's walk a ways," suggested Joe.

"It's getting dark," Frank reminded him.

"How about flashlights?"

A search of the roadster revealed that none were in it.

"I remember now," Joe said. "I put them on a shelf in the garage when I was washing the car."

It was not yet quite dark, but the early autumn twilight was deepening rapidly. The Hardy boys proceeded down the swampy trail for about a quarter of a mile, when they were forced to halt. By that time it was impossible to see more than a few feet ahead.

"I hate to give up," Frank declared. "It looks as if we've hit upon something that might be interesting. But I guess there's no use going any farther."

Reluctantly Joe agreed with him.

"We can come back again in daylight and follow up the trail," he said.

They floundered through the darkness to their car, got it turned around, and drove back to the road. In a little while they were out on the main highway, bowling swiftly along the concrete pavement leading back to Bayport.

"Something mighty queer about that whole business," mused Frank. "If the van driver didn't intend going to Spurtown, why did he ask us the way?"

"Maybe he wanted to make sure he wouldn't take the Spurtown road."

"Yet Jockey Ivan says the fellow was absolutely dependable."

"He might have been held up and forced to go up the side trail."

"That's possible. We'll go back there and follow those tracks to the finish."

It was long after dark when they arrived home. They felt confident that Aunt Gertrude would have plenty to say about their tardiness.

"Bad enough for us to go to the horse-races without being late for dinner!" chuckled Joe as they put the car in the garage. "Shall we explain why we were delayed?"

"We'd better not," Frank decided. "We may be all wrong about those tracks. They may not be those of the van after all, and we'll only make ourselves look foolish. We'd better just keep mum until we know for certain."

They hurried around to the front entrance and were just ascending the steps to the veranda, when the door opened and their chum Chet Morton stepped out.

"Hello, Chet!" cried Frank. "What's up?"

Their fat, good-humored chum wagged his head solemnly.

"Sorry I can't stay, fellows. I just dropped around to see if you were in. Gosh, I wouldn't be in your shoes for anything!"

"What's the matter?" they asked.

"It may not matter to you," said Chet, "but

it might mean a lot to some folks. Of course, you may be different.''

"What are you driving at?'' Frank demanded.

"You're wanted by the police, that's all,'' came the surprising reply.

Then, without volunteering any further information Chet hurried down the steps and disappeared in the darkness.

CHAPTER IV

THE CLAY HAND

DINNER was an agonizing meal.

Aunt Gertrude, as they had predicted, had plenty to say and was very curious to learn how much money the boys had lost by betting on the horse-races. Her nephews assured her that betting had been farthest from their thoughts, but the good lady merely sniffed dubiously.

"It's the truth," Frank declared, and then told the story of the runaway automobile.

He and Joe cast furtive glances at their father throughout the meal. Had Chet told him that they were wanted by the police?

Above all, why did the authorities want them? Was it on account of the adventure with the runaway car at the race-track that afternoon? Had the owner of the machine laid a charge against them?

"Chet was here," said Mr. Hardy finally, putting aside his table napkin.

"We—we met him," gulped Joe.

Frank had lost his appetite completely. "I

29

guess I don't care for any dessert,'' he said.

"Ate too many frankfurters at the race-track, I'll be bound," said Aunt Gertrude.

"You seem to be worrying about something," Mr. Hardy remarked blandly.

"Me? Oh, no, I have nothing to worry about," said Frank.

"I thought you might be fretting because Chet told you the police wanted you."

Joe and Frank exchanged glances.

"He told you?" muttered Joe in a faint voice.

Fenton Hardy began to laugh.

"I didn't want to spoil Chet's fun," he explained.

The two boys felt greatly relieved. So it was just one of their chum's practical jokes, after all!

"He'll be sorry for that!" Joe declared vengefully. "I was so worried I couldn't eat my dinner. Mother, I think I'll have some of that pudding after all."

"Whatever put it into his head to tell us we were wanted by the police?" Frank exclaimed.

"I did," Mr. Hardy answered. "As a matter of fact, you *are* wanted by the police."

Their spirits dropped to zero again.

"What?" gasped Frank.

"I, as a licensed private detective and a former member of the New York Police Department, want you both to go with me on a little errand tonight,'' laughed their father. ''That's being wanted by the police, isn't it?''

''Where to, Dad?'' they asked eagerly.

''I want you to go to the home of a man named Vilnoff.''

''Vilnoff!'' Frank exclaimed. ''Why, we know him. He's one of the men who was in the way of that car we told you about. Who is he, anyway?''

''He's a wealthy foreigner who rented a furnished home in Bayport a few months ago. I have a little business to discuss with him tonight, so I thought perhaps you'd like to come along.''

''Sure thing!'' Joe said.

They reached Vilnoff's home shortly after eight o'clock. Fenton Hardy said nothing to the boys about his mission, and his business with the man was brief. He merely inquired about the foreigner's whereabouts the previous afternoon.

''Why, I was at de football game at Seneca, sir,'' Vilnoff answered promptly. ''I sat by your son here.''

''You didn't mention that, Frank,'' said his father.

''It is true,'' replied the lad. ''He wanted me to explain some points about the plays.''

''That's all I wanted to know, Mr. Vilnoff,''

replied Mr. Hardy. "Thank you very much."

"It is an alibi you want, yes?"

"Just making a little check-up. Nothing serious, you understand."

Vilnoff smiled affably.

"I onnerstand pairfectly. Moreover, you fonny, inquisitive Americans will not have to bother about me any longer, because I sail for my native land in a few days."

"Oh, leaving the city, Mr. Vilnoff?"

"I leave America for good. It is too bad I will not see any more football. Your son," and Vilnoff made a polite bow in Frank's direction, "he was so good as to explain that complicated game to me. But I am stupid, yes. I do not onnerstand football. It is very rough. Very confuse."

Mr. Vilnoff bowed them out of the house, thanking them profusely for the honor they had bestowed upon him by calling. On the way back home Frank asked curiously:

"What did you want his alibi for, Dad?"

Fenton Hardy shrugged.

"Oh, the government is just checking up on all visiting aliens," he remarked casually. "It wasn't very important."

"A result of the explosion in the munitions factory?" Joe suggested shrewdly.

"I wouldn't go so far as to say that I connect Vilnoff with that," returned Mr. Hardy.

Although their father would say no more, the boys felt that they could read between the lines. They were firmly convinced that his investigations had some connection with the factory explosion. Later, when he left them to go on an errand that would take him into the downtown section of Bayport, they talked the matter over.

"There's something fishy about that Vilnoff fellow," declared Joe. "I'd like to know a little more about him."

"Same here. What say we go back there and take a look around?"

"Back to Vilnoff's house?"

"Why not? If Dad has his eye on Vilnoff there must be some mystery about him."

Acting on this sudden impulse, the lads made their way back to the foreigner's home. It was a big, luxurious dwelling with well-kept grounds and gardens. The Hardy boys slipped through the gate, stole across the lawns, and noticing a light in a basement window, crept forward to investigate.

They crouched beside the window and peered into the basement below. The room they could see seemed to have been fitted up as a workshop of some kind. A motor was running, and a man, sitting at a bench with his back toward them, was engaged in some work that demanded the use of a number of small tools. Occasionally he would reach toward a rack in front of him and take down a wrench, a small screw-driver, a tiny hammer, and other articles as he needed them.

Finally he stood up abruptly and turned a switch. The motor stopped. The man moved away from the bench, strode across the room, and snapped out the basement light when he reached the door. At no time had the boys had a glimpse of his face.

The young detectives straightened up. They were intensely interested in Mr. Vilnoff's underground machine shop, but as yet it meant nothing to them.

"Let's take a prowl around to the back of the house," suggested Frank. "Perhaps——"

Suddenly Joe gripped his arm.

"Listen!" he whispered.

On the gravel path leading from the front of the dwelling they heard crunching footsteps.

"Someone is coming!" whispered Frank. "Better hide."

They separated, and ducked into tall bushes at the side of the path. Unfortunately Frank tripped over a wire and went sprawling into the crackling brush. He heard a shout behind him, picked himself up, and broke into a run. Some distance away he could hear thudding footsteps as Joe fled toward the back of the estate.

Frank raced beneath the trees, hoping to gain

the street, but a dark figure loomed up suddenly before him. The lad dodged, but the man was too quick for him, and seized him by the arm.

"You come along with me!" growled his captor menacingly. "We don't like sneak thieves around here."

Frank struggled, but the man hustled him back across the lawn toward the house. When they reached the walk two more figures emerged from the shadows. One of them was Joe, held firmly by someone in a chauffeur's uniform.

"Did you get the other guy, Harker?" called out the driver.

"You bet I got him, and I'm hangin' onto him, too. They'll get jail for this. Better call the police and have 'em arrested."

"We'll let the boss do that. Bring 'em into the house."

The Hardy boys realized that their plight was serious. Although their actions had been the result of curiosity, there was no doubt that they had been trespassing. If Vilnoff should lay charges against them they would be in a bad fix.

The chauffeur and his companion, who seemed to be the gardener of the estate, hustled their young captives unceremoniously through a side door into a bare little room. There the driver stood guard while the other fellow went in search of Vilnoff.

As they were waiting, Joe scrutinized the chauffeur closely. He recollected his face clearly. This was indeed the man who had driven the car that had forced the Hardy boys off the road outside of Spurtown that afternoon. The boy decided he was a reckless individual.

A few minutes later Vilnoff appeared, clad in slippers and dressing gown. When he recognized the Hardy boys he turned threateningly toward his servants.

"What nonsense is this?" he snapped. "These boys are not burglars."

"Well, chief, we caught 'em prowlin' around the house," mumbled the chauffeur, "and you gave orders we was to tackle anybody actin' suspicious like, so——"

Vilnoff silenced him with an impatient gesture.

"I am very sorry," he told Frank and Joe. "My men, they have make the mistake. You will please to accept my pardon, yes?"

He ordered the servants out of the room. Then he said, "I know you are not burglars, of course. And yet, maybe there is some explanation. Perhaps you will tell me—*what* were you doing on the grounds of my home?"

The Hardy boys did not reply to the question.

"You lost somet'ing, perhaps, when you were here a little while ago?" suggested Vilnoff. "You came back to look for it, yes? Ah well, come back in de daytime. You may find it then.''

And so, bowing and smiling politely, he ushered them to the door, apologized again on behalf of his servants, and let them out.

''You will come and see me again, yes?'' said Vilnoff. ''I promise that you will not be treated like burglars a second time.''

The Hardy boys went down the walk in silence. After a while Frank spoke up.

''We were mighty lucky to get out of that jam as easily as we did.''

''I'll say so. I thought we were going to be turned over to the police. Vilnoff seems to be a pretty good scout.''

''We didn't fool him,'' Frank said. ''He was just a little too polite and agreeable to suit me. He knew perfectly well that we were spying on his house, but he just didn't want to do anything about it.''

''You think he knew?''

''All the evidence was against us, and yet he went out of his way to make up an explanation for us.''

''But why?''

''I suppose he didn't want to start any trouble. Maybe he didn't want the police called in. There's another thing that occurred to me tonight, Joe. When Dad asked him where he was yesterday afternoon he had a perfect alibi to the effect that he was at the football game and that I was sitting right by him and could substantiate the fact.''

"It was true, wasn't it?"

"Sure, but I believe he sat beside me deliberately, thinking that he would be questioned later on.''

"There may be something to that," admitted Joe thoughtfully. "He's a queer fellow, that Vilnoff. Did you notice how much he blinks, and then raises his right hand in the air every little while?"

"Nervousness, probably. Oh, well, if he's leaving the country in a day or so we won't have to worry about him.''

"By the way," Joe remarked, tugging at something in his pocket, "I didn't show you what I found near Vilnoff's house tonight just before we had to run away. I saw this lying on the ground and snatched it up as I took to my heels.''

"What is it?" asked his brother curiously.

They halted under a street light. Frank stared at the object Joe held out for his inspection.

It looked like a small human hand. On second glance Frank saw that it was merely a model in clay.

"A clay hand!" he exclaimed. "What in the world can it mean?"

CHAPTER V

THE MISSING TRUCK

"WHILE you boys were out gallivanting last night," Aunt Gertrude informed her nephews next morning, "a young man called to see you."

"Did he leave his name?" asked Joe.

"He did," the good lady replied with marked disapproval in her glance. "It seems he was one of those gambling friends of yours. It's bad enough going to horse-races without making friends with every Tom, Dick and Harry around the place. At least that's *my* opinion. Not that it counts for anything around this house."

"Was he Tom or Dick?" asked Frank.

"Or Harry?" Joe inquired innocently.

Aunt Gertrude glared at them.

"He said his name was Ivan. One of those jockey persons, I believe."

The Hardy boys were interested.

"Ivan, eh!" said Frank. "I wonder why he wanted to see us?"

"Perhaps he has had some news about *Topnotch*," Joe suggested.

"He had a message for you," Aunt Gertrude

said. "I told him, of course, that I would be very glad to hear what he had to say and that I would tell you about it when you came in. But he was very rude. Said he would come back this morning and give you the message himself."

Frank and Joe waited all morning in the hope that Ivan would show up, but the jockey did not appear.

"If he had something so important for us to hear, he should have been here by this time," said Frank during lunch.

"Maybe he's been in an accident. I suggest that we go over to Spurtown this afternoon and look him up. After all, we don't want to waste the whole day. I'd like to do a little more sleuthing along that old road."

"That's right. We'll take the car and run over to Spurtown."

When they got the auto out they discovered engine trouble, which necessitated their taking the roadster to the corner garage for repairs. The mechanic who investigated the trouble told them that the work could not be completed until late that afternoon.

"In that case we'll have to go to Spurtown by bus," said Frank.

When they arrived at the race-track, they asked among the jockeys about Ivan, but apparently he had not been seen in the vicinity

since the previous day. Further inquiries revealed the fact that *Topnotch* was still missing,
and that the mystery surrounding the disappearance of the race-horse remained as deep as
ever.

"I hope Ivan hasn't been kidnaped too," Joe
remarked. "It seems queer that he didn't come
to see us this morning as he said he would."

The boys got a lift from a friendly motorist
who drove them as far as the crossroads. Then
they set out on foot to follow the old trail they
had investigated the previous afternoon. Before they had gone very far, however, Frank
suggested that they might save time by taking
a short-cut through a field beside the road.

"If we cross the field we'll come out somewhere near the spot where we had to leave the
car last night," he stated.

"Anything that saves walking will suit me,"
Joe answered, promptly beginning to climb the
wooden fence. Then suddenly he was held fast.

"Good gosh! Barbed wire!" he exclaimed.
"I didn't see it."

"No wonder. It's half hidden."

A strand of the metal ran along the top of
the fence and Joe's trousers had become firmly
snagged just when he was halfway over.

"I'm glad you went first," chuckled Frank.
"Now I'll know enough to crawl *under* the
barrier."

Joe, trying to balance himself across the top rail, was making an effort to release his trousers from the spikes when he suddenly lost his balance and toppled over. There was a rending, tearing sound, and by the time the lad sat up he saw that he had left a substantial portion of his pants on the jagged wire.

Frank was laughing hilariously at his brother's plight—so much so, in fact, that he failed to notice that another strand of barbed wire ran along the under side of the fence.

R-r-r-ip! Frank scrambled through, crestfallen to discover that the sharp points had torn a jagged rent in the back of his coat.

"Maybe we'll save time by crossing this field," observed Joe disconsolately, trying to survey the damage to his trousers, "but it is mighty hard on clothes." Then, with a grin when he saw that Frank had not escaped scot-free, he added, "Aunt Gertrude would probably tell you that 'he laughs best who laughs last!' "

They continued their journey across the field. They were not halfway to the opposite enclosure when they discovered that they were not alone on the property. About fifty yards ahead they spied a flock of goats grazing peacefully. The animals raised their heads and looked at the boys.

"If there is a billy goat in that outfit I hope he has a quiet disposition," observed Frank.

There *was* such a creature in the flock. It moved a little apart from the other animals, gazing at the intruders with marked suspicion. Then, with a bleat of wrath, he began trotting toward them.

"Run for it!" yelled Joe.

The boys raced for the fence. Seeing them in flight, the animal lowered its head and set out in pursuit.

Joe reached the fence first and cleared it at one bound. Frank got over it too, but was given considerable assistance by the goat, who arrived there almost simultaneously. He went sailing over the low fence and landed sprawling in a thicket. The creature then uttered a bleat of triumph and walked away.

"Whew! What a race!" gasped Joe, fanning himself with his hat. "Are you hurt?"

Frank crawled out of the bushes, rubbing himself.

"Only my dignity!" he answered. "Gosh, I never knew a goat could travel so fast."

"I never thought we could, either. We'd cross the line first at any Bayport High track meet if we could keep up that pace all the time. I'll bet we broke every record for the hundred-yard dash."

"Somebody better put up a 'danger' sign here, too," suggested Frank.

Slightly shaken by their mishaps, the boys

continued on their way, crossing through the thickets for a little distance and eventually coming to the abandoned road they had followed the previous evening. In the daylight they were able to distinguish the heavy tracks more clearly, and followed them for several hundred feet from the place where they had been obliged to give up their former search.

Suddenly the ruts branched off from the road altogether, and led directly into the brush and shrubbery. On a nearby tree the lads saw a placard, which read:

"Danger—Keep Out—Target Practice."

The Hardy boys were in no mood to quit now.

"I can't hear any shooting," remarked Joe. "Let's push on."

"I don't believe in signs anyway," returned his brother. "At least not that one."

"Do you think it was put there just to keep people away?"

"If *Topnotch* is hidden in this shrubbery, then this marker may have been put there just to frighten off any searchers."

The ruts led down a sort of rough trail from which trees had been cleared away. It looked like an abandoned road originally cut through by settlers, or a right-of-way hacked through the forest for a power transmission line.

Suddenly from around a bend in the trail just ahead there bounded a huge dog. It was

a vicious looking animal, and when it saw the
boys, stood stock-still for a moment, growling
ferociously.

The Hardy boys halted.

"I don't like the looks of this," muttered Joe.

Frank tried to win the animal's friendship.
He whistled to it and patted his knee invitingly.

"Come on, old fellow!" he said.

The dog was distinctly hostile. With an angry snarl it suddenly broke into a run, heading
directly toward the lads, its teeth bared.

Frank and Joe did not remain to argue the
matter, but leaped from the trail, each picking
out a substantial looking oak which they climbed
hastily to safety. The dog, barking loudly,
rushed from one tree to the other, leaping and
clawing at the trunks.

It was an awkward predicament. The worst
part of it was the dog showed no disposition to
go away, and finally sat down growling at the
foot of the tree in which Joe had taken refuge.

"Treed like a couple of raccoons!" grumbled
Joe bitterly.

The woods were very thick, and Frank
noticed that a heavy branch of another tree
was within reach of the one upon which he
was perched. This gave him an idea. He gripped the other limb, swung out on it, and hauled
himself hand-over-hand until he came within
reach of a branch of still another tree.

"Come on!" he called to his brother.

This Joe did, but the dog saw what his prospective victims were doing and stood his ground, barking furiously.

"Reminds me of a couple of apes!" Joe laughed, swinging himself over into the boughs of a huge oak.

In this manner, crawling, swinging, and leaping, the Hardy boys penetrated deeper and deeper into the woods while the frantic beast below them circled about in the undergrowth. The lads' hope that the animal might lose itself was in vain. They could hear the snapping of twigs and the crackling of leaves all too clearly.

"What's worrying me," panted Joe, as he sat in the crotch of a huge bough to rest, "is how we're ever going to find our way out of this woods even if we do get rid of the dog."

Through the foliage Frank noticed a little clearing straight ahead. He swung himself into the next tree to get a better view. As he did so, he uttered a yell of astonishment.

"We've found it, Joe! I can see the van!"

CHAPTER VI

THERE, in a secluded little clearing in the very heart of the forest, stood the van that had passed them the afternoon they had driven to the football game at Seneca.

Frank could see it quite plainly now. He was so excited by the discovery that he called out to his brother, forgetting that the closed truck might be occupied. When he realized what he had done he crouched down, watching to see if anyone had been alarmed by his shout.

No one appeared, however, so he swung his way through the branches until he reached a heavy limb that extended directly over the top of the van. A few minutes later Joe joined his brother. Frank dropped to the roof of the big vehicle, and the younger Hardy soon followed.

Their enemy, the dog, had not been shaken off. He scrambled through the thickets and set up a terrific barking when he came in sight of his quarry.

"Some watch dog!" fumed Joe.

47

The rear door of the van was open, otherwise the lads might have been trapped on the roof. As it was, they were able to swing themselves down into the truck. The floor was not sufficiently near the ground to permit the dog to reach them, despite its frenzied leaps.

With the exception of a heap of old horse blankets in a corner the place was empty. There were a pail and a curry-comb, sufficient indication that the truck certainly had been used for the transportation of a horse.

Frank had not forgotten his flashlight this time. He played the beam on a dark corner near the front of the vehicle, and suddenly pounced upon something lying on the floor.

"What have you found?" asked Joe.

The object was merely a cardboard tag, yet it was important, for on it was written:

TOPNOTCH
PRESCOTT STABLES

There was no further doubt in their minds now. They were surely on the trail of the missing race-horse!

Suddenly the dog's barking ceased. In the distance the Hardy boys heard a sharp whistle, and a voice call out:

"Here, Rusty!"

The animal abruptly left its siege of the van

and rushed across the clearing, to disappear in the bushes.

"Someone is coming!" snapped Frank, as he hurriedly closed the door. "Get under those blankets!"

The boys dived toward the corner, sprawled out, and pulled the wool coverings over themselves. They were none too soon, for a few moments later they heard someone walking across the clearing.

"Down, Rusty!" growled a voice presently. "What's the matter? Why did you raise all that racket?"

The newcomer was standing at the back of the truck. The Hardys heard a creaking noise as he pulled open the door. Presumably he peered inside and satisfied himself that the van was empty, for he said, "Nothing in here, you crazy hound! Must have been a squirrel you were chasing."

Frank and Joe waited in an agony of suspense. Finally, to their relief, they heard the man's footsteps retreating across the clearing.

"Come on, Rusty!" growled the stranger.

Then a dead silence fell over everything once more. Frank and Joe took no chances on being discovered, however. They waited a full five minutes longer before they dared venture out from beneath the blankets.

They thoroughly examined the truck and the

clearing where the van had been abandoned, but could find nothing in the way of a clue to *Topnotch*. Frank searched in the hope of seeing the hoof-prints of the horse, but the clearing was unmarked save for the deep ruts made by the van itself.

"Well, that proves one thing, anyhow," he announced. "*Topnotch* wasn't brought here in the truck."

"Right. The horse was removed at some other place and then the machine was driven into the woods and hidden here."

Nothing was to be gained by remaining in the clearing any longer. If the boys could only locate the man who had visited the van and called the dog away they felt that they might be on the track to the solution of the mystery. Yet, when they set out to attempt to pick up his trail, they found themselves completely baffled. The barking of the dog could be heard no longer, and after half an hour's futile search the lads were forced to give up their quest.

The problem of getting back to the main road now faced them, and they solved it by following the tracks of the van until at last they reached the spot where they had parked their car the previous day. It was almost dark before they finally reached the crossroads and set out on foot toward the main Bayport highway, where they could find a bus to the city.

The Hardy boys were foot-sore and tired by the time they came in sight of such a conveyance. To their disgust it was just pulling away from the front of a service station and refreshment stand. They hurried out, waving and shouting, but the driver took no notice of them. In a moment the vehicle was speeding off toward Bayport, its tail-light twinkling ironically in the gloom.

"Now we'll have to wait another half hour," grumbled Joe. "What a break! We haven't had any luck at all today."

"I'm hungry. Let's go over to the service station and see if we can dig up something to eat."

The place in question was small and shabby, with a tiny lunch room at one side. The proprietor, a stout, sour-looking individual named Gus doubled in the rôle of cook and waiter. When Frank and Joe asked for soda and sandwiches he merely nodded indifferently and disappeared into the kitchen.

The boys waited several minutes, but still there was no sign of the sandwiches. Frank filled in the time by telephoning home to notify his mother that he and Joe might be late to dinner. At length Gus appeared with some food that was far from appetizing looking. The bottles of soda he offered were warm.

The boys were just finishing this excuse for

a meal when a truck, painted green, pulled up in front of the service station and a stout fellow in overalls climbed out. He came into the lunch room and flung his gloves on the counter.

"Hello, Gus!" he shouted. "Well, I went over there——"

The proprietor silenced him with a look, and then came over to the boys' table.

"You fellows about finished?" he demanded roughly.

"Yes," answered Frank.

"O.K., then. Pay up and beat it. This ain't no waitin' room."

"I wouldn't call it a restaurant, either," returned Frank, handing the man some change.

"If there's nothin' else you want, clear out," ordered Gus in a surly voice.

"Nice, hospitable fellow, isn't he?" remarked Joe as the brothers stepped outside. "Won't even let us wait inside until the bus comes along."

"There's something queer about that place," Frank said. "Gus wanted to talk to that driver but he didn't want to be overheard."

The boy stepped over to the green truck, glanced at the license plates, and jotted down the number on the back of an envelope. Through the windows of the lunch room the boys could see the two men in earnest conversation. It was quite dark now so the Hardys had no fear of being seen by the burly proprietor as long as they remained in the shadows and outside the ring of light from the gasoline standards.

They edged closer to the windows. One of them was partly open, and through it they heard the driver say:

"I tell you, the sign didn't work."

"Did you go in, Pete?" asked Gus.

"Sure, I went in anyway. Told me I'd lose my job! Huh! They wouldn't dare. I could tell plenty. Why, listen——"

"Not so loud, Pete," cautioned the proprietor.

The truckman lowered his voice, and the boys could distinguish nothing further of the conversation. Then the Bayport bus came rolling down the highway and pulled up to a stop in front of the service station. The Hardys quickly got aboard and the vehicle drove away.

There were only a few passengers. Among them Frank noticed a familiar face. It was that of their jockey acquaintance.

"Hello, there," said Ivan. He got up from his seat and pointed to the rear where all the places were unoccupied. "Let's go back there. I've something to tell you. I was just on my way to Bayport to call on you fellows."

CHAPTER VII

"You came to see us last night, didn't you?" asked Joe.

"Yes. I said I would be back today but I couldn't make it until now," Ivan replied.

"Is it about *Topnotch?*" inquired Frank eagerly.

The jockey nodded.

"Mr. Prescott—he's owner of *Topnotch* and the Prescott Stables, got a letter yesterday. I thought you fellows might like to hear about it, seeing you're in the detective line."

"What was in it?"

"The horse was stolen, all right. This message said *Topnotch* would be returned safe and sound if Mr. Prescott would pay a ransom."

"How much?"

"Twenty-five thousand dollars!" exclaimed the jockey.

Frank whistled in amazement.

"That's a whale of a lot of money. Is the horse worth that much?"

"He stands to win all of that and perhaps

more in a single season. Oh, yes, the horse is worth that amount all right.''

"Is Mr. Prescott going to pay it?''

"I think so. He isn't a wealthy man, and it may mean that he will have to sell some of his other horses to raise the sum, but I believe he will do it. I hope so, anyhow. Just let me get *Topnotch* back and we'll win the twenty-five thousand back soon enough.''

"How is the money to be paid over?'' inquired Joe.

"I don't know any of the details. Mr. Prescott simply told me that he had received a ransom letter. The kidnapers threatened to injure the horse so that he'll never run again unless the money is given to them. Mr. Prescott will pay all right,'' said Ivan confidently. "He wouldn't have anything happen to *Topnotch* for all the money on earth.''

At this juncture one of the passengers who had been sitting in the front of the bus moved down the aisle and took a rear seat immediately ahead of the boys. He was an undersized, shifty-eyed looking fellow and when the Hardys continued their conversation with Ivan they noticed that the stranger was obviously listening.

"Maybe your father can locate *Topnotch*,'' remarked Ivan. "I think Mr. Prescott has a notion of calling him in on the case.''

"Dad has been pretty busy on some other matters of late," Joe remarked non-committally.

"Oh, well, I think Mr. Prescott is resigned to paying the money. It's a relief to know that the horse is unharmed, at any rate."

"Perhaps you had better tell the owner to hold up payment for a day or so," Frank whispered, not wishing the stranger to hear his remark. "We've been doing a little sleuthing on the case ourselves."

Ivan, excited, said aloud, "You've been hunting for *Topnotch?* Find out anything?"

The bus was slowing down for a stop just inside the Bayport city limits. The man in the seat ahead got up. Abruptly he turned toward the boys.

"I vould say to you," he told them in a voice with a heavy accent, "that you should keep quiet about dat horse and have not'ing to do wit' such matters." With this cryptic warning he turned, hurried down the aisle, and jumped from the bus into the darkness.

Joe, Frank and Ivan were astounded at this strange interruption. Frank sprang to the window and tried to get another glimpse of the man, but he had vanished into the night and the bus was pulling away from the stop.

"What did he mean?" exclaimed the jockey, puzzled.

"He must know something about the affair," Frank said tersely.

Joe shook his head.

"He wouldn't be foolish enough to give himself away like that. I think he was just a busybody butting in. Maybe he thought he was giving us good advice by telling us to keep out of any sort of kidnaping affair."

Frank was not convinced, however, and stuck to his opinion that the foreigner's words were deliberately meant as a warning. It seemed that he was justified in this belief, for after the boys had left Jockey Ivan and gone home that evening the telephone rang. When Joe answered it he heard a sinister, menacing voice.

"You one of the Hardy boys?"

"Why, yes——"

"O.K. You've been putting your nose into this *Topnotch* affair. I'm just calling up to warn you and your brother to lay off, get me? Stay out of that business and don't even talk about it or you'll run into a lot of trouble. Understand, now! You two fellows mind your own business if you know what's healthy for you."

"Who is speaking?" Joe demanded.

"Try and find out," jeered the voice. "Keep mixing up in this *Topnotch* business and you'll know soon enough."

There was a click as the unknown caller hung up the receiver. Joe's face was solemn when he returned to the living room.

"Who was that?" asked Aunt Gertrude inquisitively.

"Oh—just some man."

The good lady snorted.

"I'm a lot the wiser," she said, and her knitting needles flashed wickedly.

When the boys went up to their room a little later Joe told Frank about the mysterious telephone warning.

"I'll bet that stranger we saw on the bus had something to do with it," the latter declared. "Well, if he thinks we're to be frightened off that easily he's mistaken. Now we'll get down to some *real* work on the case."

Next morning Chet Morton arrived at the Hardy home before the boys had finished their breakfast. Chet, stout and jolly, was known throughout Bayport for his love of fun and food.

"How now, my hearties!" he exclaimed, as he entered the dining room. "I beseech a boon of thee."

He calmly picked up an orange from a plate and began to peel it.

"Come down to earth," said Joe. "Talk twentieth century American. You mean you want us to do you a favor."

"Name it," said Frank.

"A traveler from a distant city cometh winging his way through the air—to wit, my cousin Bill, a goodly egg. I fain would journey forth to meet him, but lo, I lacketh a boat."

"What *is* all this rigmarole about?" demanded Joe.

"In other words," grinned Chet, "will you run me to the airport in your motorboat so I can meet my cousin? He's coming in by plane this morning. Surely I have made myself clear."

He popped a piece of the orange into his mouth and began munching at it with vast satisfaction.

"Take you over to the airport?" said Frank. "Sure thing. When do you want to go?"

"Forsooth, and I would fain depart at once if not sooner, ere perchance my cousin William should descend from the clouds with no one to bid him welcome to our city."

"I wish you would descend from the clouds and talk plain English," said Joe. "Come on, Frank. We'll take Shakespeare Junior over to the airport, and if he bursts into any more of that lingo we'll dump him over the side of the boat into the bay."

"Fair enough," Frank agreed.

The boys went down High Street toward the bay and unlocked the door of their boat-house.

Their craft, the *Sleuth,* was a fast, trim little affair that had been purchased with the reward money they had received for solving a mystery of considerable importance a year or so before.

The Bayport flying field was on the banks of the Willow River which ran into Barmet Bay, an indentation of the Atlantic Coast. The airport, therefore, could be reached both by land and by water.

"How long is your cousin going to stay with you, Chet?" asked Frank, as he opened the door of the boat-house.

"About a month, I think. He comes from a little town up in New England, but has been in New York. I haven't seen him for several years. He's a nice fellow. I think you'll like him."

The boys stepped into the craft and Joe started the engine. In a few minutes they were speeding rapidly down the bay. About a quarter of a mile out they noticed a speed-boat drumming in their wake.

Although the *Sleuth* was one of the fastest launches on the bay, this new arrival overhauled them and went flashing by in a smother of foam. Frank and Joe noticed a familiar looking figure seated in the stern.

"Why, that looks like Mr. Vilnoff!" Joe exclaimed.

"I wonder where he's headed for?" Frank gasped.

It was soon apparent that the speed-boat was steering for their own destination, as it cut across the bay toward the mouth of the Willow River and went roaring in the direction of the airport. The *Sleuth* was soon left far behind.

"Makes our little craft look like a rowboat in comparison," Frank laughed.

As they were traveling up the river they saw a plane ascend above the airport. It circled to gain altitude, then straightened out and droned off.

"Looks like the New York plane taking off," observed Chet.

"Perhaps that's where Vilnoff is going," Joe said. "Remember, Frank, he said the other night that he would be leaving the country in a few days."

The three chums reached the dock at the foot of the path leading up the slope to the flying field, tied the boat and went on to the airport. The plane from New York was due in a few minutes.

Soon they spied it, a mere speck in the sky. Then it grew larger. They could hear the drumming of the motors as the machine swiftly roared toward the field. It banked, then came down in a long, graceful glide, settled on the field, and taxied toward the airport office and waiting room. When it came to a full stop an attendant placed a portable step beneath the door of the big machine and the passengers began to emerge. The first to alight was a chubby, good-natured looking lad of about seventeen, so like Chet Morton in appearance that the boys knew at once that he was the visiting cousin from New England.

"Hi, Bill!" shouted Chet.

"Hello, Chet," grinned the newcomer, hurrying over to shake hands. "Nice of you to meet me."

Bill Morton was introduced to the Hardy boys, who liked him at once.

"Mighty glad to meet you," said Frank.

"We'll help show you a good time," added Joe.

Then Frank and Joe received a distinct surprise. From out of the plane stepped their father, accompanied by a tall, distinguished looking stranger. Fenton Hardy was quite as astonished to see his sons at the airport as they were to see him. They knew that he had not been at home the previous night, but they were accustomed to his sudden and mysterious comings and goings.

"Hello, boys!" he said, smiling. "Did you come to meet me? How did you know I would be on this plane? I'd like you to meet my client, Mr. Howe. Mr. Howe, my boys—Frank and Joe.''

The lads shook hands with the stranger and then explained their presence at the airport. Mr. Hardy laughed.

''I wondered,'' he said. ''I thought I had kept my movements pretty secret.'' He drew his sons aside and said quietly, ''I've just been in New York seeing our friend Vilnoff. He is sailing for Europe today.''

''Vilnoff!'' exclaimed Frank in amazement. ''You couldn't have seen him in New York, Dad. He just left here by plane a few minutes ago.''

Fenton Hardy looked bewildered.

''Impossible! I was talking to him in New York this morning.''

''And we're positive he came down the bay in a speed-boat just in time to catch the New York plane!'' Joe declared.

CHAPTER VIII

A SUSPICIOUS DRIVER

Fenton Hardy was deeply concerned.

"This is an awkward mix-up. I can't understand it," he said. "I must know who is who in this affair. You must do something for me at once."

"What is it, Dad?" asked Frank eagerly.

"Vilnoff said he would sail on the *Atlantis* this morning." Mr. Hardy glanced at his watch. "It's due to leave New York in an hour. I have an important conference with Mr. Howe and some other people just now so I'll have to leave this matter in your hands."

"How can we make sure that Vilnoff sailed?" Joe inquired.

"Get in touch by telephone with the Quickshot Photo Company in New York," said the detective guardedly. He groped in his pocket and handed them a card. "You'll find the address here. Instruct them, on my behalf, to rush a cameraman down to the dock and take moving pictures of all the passengers that board the *Atlantis* before she sails."

"All right, Dad!" responded Frank. "Come on, Joe. Let's get busy."

The airplane company provided transportation for their passengers between Bayport and the flying field, so Chet and his cousin said they would go on to the Morton home at once. Fenton Hardy and Mr. Howe also hurried off, leaving Frank and Joe to their problem of conveying instructions immediately to the Quickshot people.

They hurried into the waiting room. There were only two telephone booths. One of them was occupied, and just as the lads were rushing toward the other, an enormously fat man waddled into the compartment just ahead of them. He did not get inside without difficulty.

"I'll help you," cried Joe, and gave the obese person a push that got him safely through the small opening. Far from being appreciative of the assistance, the stout gentleman pulled the door shut with a bang and glared at the lad sourly through the glass.

In a moment the young man in the next compartment showed signs of finishing his conversation. The boys took up their position outside so as to be next in line. The speaker put back the receiver, opened the door, and stepped from the booth.

"Go ahead," said Joe to his brother. "Got the number?"

Just as Frank was about to enter, a fussy old lady armed with an umbrella, and carrying several parcels and a large basket, suddenly appeared. She said, "Thank you, boys! Do you mind holding these for a moment?" and calmly handed Frank the basket and Joe her bundles. Then she stepped into the compartment, closed the door, sat down, and leisurely began thumbing through the telephone book.

"Of all the colossal nerve!" exclaimed Joe indignantly. "Just when we are in a hurry, too!"

The fat man appeared to have settled down to an interminable stay in the next booth. Then the old lady, after finding her number, discovered she could not locate any change. She began a laborious search through her purse until she found the necessary coins.

"This is fierce!" said Frank, hopping about with impatience. Ten minutes had already passed.

"We'll never get in touch with the Quickshot people in time," groaned Joe.

The fat man, however, eventually wedged himself out. Frank lost no time getting inside the booth, while Joe stood on guard over the old lady's belongings. In less than a minute the Quickshot office was on the wire and had received the instructions.

"O. K.!" said the office manager. "We'll

send a man down there right away and forward the films to Mr. Hardy.''

Their mission accomplished, the boys breathed a sigh of relief and left the waiting room. They returned to the dock, got into their boat, and started for Bayport.

''Hope there won't be any slip-up about those movies,'' said Frank.

Halfway home the boys spied a launch drifting sluggishly in the ripples. There were two men in the craft, one of whom appeared to be toiling at a stalled engine. The other, standing by, waved his arms frantically as the boys came nearer.

''Help us,'' he called.

Frank brought the *Sleuth* alongside. To the surprise of the Hardy boys they discovered that the man signaling for help was none other than Gus, proprietor of the service station where they had waited for the bus the previous night.

''Will you take me to Bayport?'' cried the burly fellow. ''I hired this launch, but the engine has stalled and I'm in a hurry.''

''It'll take me half an hour to fix this,'' grumbled the boatman.

''Hop in,'' Frank said, grasping the side of the craft.

Evidently Gus had not recognized the boys. He climbed into the *Sleuth,* and in a moment they were pulling away from the disabled boat.

"How about letting her out to full speed?" suggested Gus. "I'm in a mighty big hurry."

Frank winked at his brother.

"I may," he answered, "on one condition."

Gus looked puzzled. "What do you mean?" he asked.

"What's the secret of that gas station you manage? We stopped by there for something to eat last night and it seemed to us that you don't welcome customers very heartily."

Gus now recognized the boys, and became flustered.

"Why—why, I guess I must have been busy," he stammered.

"You didn't seem to be when we were there."

"Well—I'm sorry—I was expecting a man on business—it must have been on my mind," said Gus lamely, and the boys could see that the man would volunteer no information about his place of work.

Frank opened up the throttle, and the *Sleuth* fairly leaped through the waves as it rushed toward Bayport. When it reached the boat-house the man thanked the lads for their help and apologized again for his conduct on the previous night. Then he hurried off. Joe, watching him, saw him climb into a green truck that was waiting at the corner.

"Doesn't that look like Pete's truck?"

The big machine lumbered away from the corner and rumbled down the street.

"I'd like to know a little more about Gus and his friend Pete," observed Frank.

"I'll bet they're up to some shady business," commented Joe. "We'll look 'em up. Right now we'd better get home. You remember what's on for tonight."

The Hardy boys had been invited to a dance at a girls' school which was located on the Willow River, some distance beyond the airport. As the evening was clear they decided to make the journey in the *Sleuth*. They had a very good time at the party, and reluctantly said good-bye to their friends about half-past eleven.

They had not traveled half a mile toward home before their motor began to balk. A few kicks and splutters, and it died down altogether.

"Now what's wrong?" grumbled Frank, picking up the flashlight and examining the engine.

"I know," said Joe in a rueful voice. "It's my fault. I guess I'm getting absent-minded."

"Don't tell me you forgot to fill her up with gas before we set out."

"That's exactly what happened."

The boat drifted sluggishly in the current.

"Now we're in a fine fix!" said Frank. "I

suppose there's nothing else to do but let her drift ashore, tie her up, and walk home by the airport road. My feet are sore enough from dancing, without walking a long stretch. I ought to make you carry me.''

The Willow River was not very wide, and the current was propelling them toward a point of land which they could discern vaguely through the gloom. They waited patiently until at last the bow of the boat grated on the shore. As it did so, they heard the muffled beat of a motor.

"Listen!" whispered Joe.

They saw a dark shape approaching them on the water. It proved to be a big launch moving swiftly and almost silently in their direction. There was something sinister about the rapid, stealthy progress of the other boat. The boys remained quiet as mice.

Apparently they had not been noticed. The other craft nosed in toward the shore about fifty yards away. Then the Hardys saw a light flash, followed by a murmur of voices.

"Maybe those fellows can lend us some gas," said Frank. "I'm going over to talk to them."

He got out of the boat and began to make his way up the shore in the darkness. His footfalls made no noise in the soft sand. As he drew closer to the other launch he could see several men moving up the beach.

"Careful now!" he heard a voice say. "We've got to be mighty quiet about this job. Get those cases up into the woods as fast as you can."

Frank halted. As his eyes grew accustomed to the gloom he saw that several men were unloading a number of heavy boxes from the motorboat. They were carrying them up the beach toward the dark woods that lay about fifty feet from the edge of the water.

As the boy watched, a member of the group turned on a flashlight. Its glare fell full upon one of them who was depositing a large case in the sand. He straightened up, and shouted in a rasping voice:

"Turn off that light, you fool! Do you want to have us all caught?"

Frank gasped. The beam of the flashlight had revealed the speaker as Pete, the truck-driver who had called on Gus at the service station. If the Hardy boy had any doubt about the man's identity it was removed when the fellow with the flashlight said:

"O. K., Pete. I didn't think."

"You'd better think!" growled the burly driver. "We don't want anybody coming down here to nose around and ask us what we're doing. Hurry up, now, and get that case on your shoulders. Carry it to the truck."

The other man hastily lifted up one of the

boxes and trudged off into the woods. Frank waited no longer. Noiselessly he hurried back to the *Sleuth*.

"What's up?" asked Joe. "Didn't they give you any gas?"

"Sh!" his brother cautioned him. "We've stumbled onto something, Joe. Our friend Pete and a gang of men are unloading stuff secretly from that launch and taking it into the woods."

"Let's follow them," urged the younger Hardy without a moment's hesitation.

"Come on, then."

The boys stole down the shore, but by the time they got near the mysterious launch the workers had disappeared. Frank discovered a path which led into the woods. The boys struck off down this trail, confident that the men were not far ahead of them.

The Hardys proceeded cautiously into the heavy gloom of the woods. At length they spied a gleam of red light some distance ahead. They waited a while, but could hear no voices, and could see nothing of the men.

"That must be the tail-light of the truck Pete meant," Frank decided. "We'll move up a little closer."

Soon the big machine loomed just ahead of them. The red gleam illuminated the license plate, and Frank stooped down to examine it.

The number corresponded with that on the green truck Pete had left parked outside the service station.

"That's his machine, all right," said Frank.

As he spoke, he heard a muffled cry from Joe. Frank wheeled around, just in time to catch a glimpse of his brother struggling in the grasp of two men. Another stranger plunged out from among the trees, hurled himself on Frank, and bore the lad to the ground.

CHAPTER IX

MR. PRESCOTT

THE Hardy boys had been taken completely by surprise. They struggled valiantly, but were no match for their captors. Their eyes were quickly blindfolded, their arms and legs bound with rope.

"I guess they must have seen that light and it made them curious," growled Pete. "Dump 'em back of the bushes while we finish this job."

Frank and Joe were thrown unceremoniously on the ground beside the road. They could see nothing, but they judged that the men were completing their task of loading the truck. At length they heard Pete say:

"That'll do. Now let's beat it out of here."

"How about those boys?"

"Leave 'em be. We'll be far enough away from here by the time they get loose. Serves 'em right for bein' so nosey."

The roar of the motor drowned out the men's voices, and a moment later the Hardys could hear the vehicle rumbling off down the road.

"A nice mess we got ourselves into!" Joe

muttered in disgust as he struggled in his
efforts to undo the ropes.

"We're lucky it isn't worse," said Frank
"If Pete had recognized us we wouldn't have
escaped so easily."

"I don't call this being let off easily, bound
and blindfolded and thrown on the ground,"
said Joe.

Frank wriggled around until he was lying
with his back to his brother. Then, as he
groped about, his fingers found the knots of
the rope that tied Joe's wrists. After a few
minutes' tugging and pulling he managed to
undo one of them. The others came easily, and
it was not long before the boy's hands were
free. He whipped off the blindfold, hastily un-
tied the ropes from his ankles, and busied himself with freeing Frank.

"We didn't distinguish ourselves that time,"
the older lad said. "Score one for Mr. Pete.
I'd certainly like to know what was in those
cases."

"We're not likely to find out now. The best
thing we can do is to get home."

"Without gas?" Frank reminded him.

"I forgot. What shall we do? Walk?"

"Let's go back and see if their launch is still
at the beach."

They retraced their steps down the road to
the river. The boat in which Pete and his

companions had arrived had left by this time, however. Apparently one man had remained to take charge of it while the others accompanied the cargo in the truck.

The Hardy boys made a welcome discovery just the same, in the form of a gallon can almost filled with gasoline. Apparently it had been taken out of the launch and overlooked by the men when they had left.

"This is a break, anyway!" declared Frank gleefully, holding up the can. "We won't have to walk home after all."

They lost no time replenishing the fuel supply of the *Sleuth,* and soon were speeding down the river and out into Barmet Bay. Their sturdy craft putted swiftly toward the twinkling lights of Bayport. It was half-past two by Frank's watch when they reached the boathouse.

"We'll surely get a lecture if we waken Aunt Gertrude at this hour of the morning!" said Joe. "I hope the door isn't locked. We haven't a house key."

They hurried up High Street, and found their home in total darkness. Quietly the boys stole up onto the veranda and tried the door. It was locked.

"I dare you to ring the bell!" said Frank.

"Nothing doing. I'll sleep in the garage first," returned his brother.

"No need of that. Let's climb up to the roof of the porch, and crawl through the window of our own room."

"That's an idea."

In a moment the boys were shinning up the pillars of the veranda. They grasped the ledge and hauled themselves up onto the roof. Here another setback awaited them; the window of their room was closed and locked.

The only one open was that leading to Aunt Gertrude's quarters. It was halfway up. Did they dare run the risk of disturbing their eccentric relative?

"I'm game if you are," Frank whispered.

"You go first," said his brother in stifled tones.

Frank crept along the roof. If luck were with them they might be able to enter Aunt Gertrude's room and gain the hallway beyond without awakening her.

Gently Frank reached out to raise the window a little higher. He almost tumbled off the roof in surprise as he did so, for a white figure suddenly appeared in front of him. A pistol was thrust through the open space and pointed at his chest.

"Get away from here this minute or I'll shoot!"

It was Aunt Gertrude, standing there in curling papers and a voluminous cotton nightgown.

"It's only Frank," her nephew assured her hastily. "Don't shoot!"

"Who?" she demanded.

"Your nephew, Frank. Joe and I couldn't get in."

Aunt Gertrude glared at the boys.

"Brats!" she snapped. "Come in off that roof. I'm a nervous wreck. I might have killed you if—if——"

Frank reached out and took the pistol from his aunt's fingers. He was fearful it might go off.

There was no danger, however! It was only a toy gun. Although the joke had been on the boys, they now used it to tease their relative.

"Where did you get this, Aunt Gertrude?" Frank asked as he crawled through the window, followed by Joe.

"I—I keep it under my pillow—for protection," quavered the lady, furious that her deception had been found out.

Joe could not repress a snicker. Aunt Gertrude grabbed the toy pistol from Frank's hand and thrust it under her pillow.

"Get out of here!" she ordered wrathfully. "The very idea! Climbing in through my window in the middle of the night. It's lucky I didn't drop dead of heart failure. Leave the room this very instant and go to bed. I'll have something to say to your mother about this in the morning, my fine young gentlemen.''

"We'll tell her you pointed a toy gun at us,'' chuckled Frank, as the pair hustled out of the good lady's room. She slammed the door behind them with a bang.

For once the boys had a joke on their temperamental aunt. Moreover, she never said a word about their unorthodox manner of entering the house.

The moment Frank and Joe awakened the following morning, they began to discuss the events on the river the evening before.

"We started out to find *Topnotch* and now we've stumbled upon another kind of mystery,'' was the way Frank summed up the situation.

"Let's stick to the *Topnotch* affair,'' Joe said. "We've made some progress on that case by locating the van.''

The boys had no additional success during the next few days. They scanned the papers eagerly every morning for word of the missing race-horse, but learned nothing new. They could not even find any mention of a search being made for the animal. At length, becoming impatient, they set out for Spurtown and looked up Ivan, the jockey, whom they found at the race-track.

"No, *Topnotch* isn't back yet,'' he told them in answer to their inquiries.

Mr. Prescott, owner of the horse, had been

in communication with the kidnapers, he said. His method of replying to them was by means of "personal" advertisements inserted in the Spurtown newspaper.

"He has just about decided to pay the ransom, but of course he wants to be sure that the men actually have the horse," Ivan said. "That is the hitch now. He is demanding proof from them that the animal will be returned unharmed if he hands over the money. By the way, Mr. Prescott is coming to Bayport tomorrow. I'll tell him to call on you."

Ivan was as good as his word. Next morning a lanky, kindly-faced old gentleman with white mustache and goatee called at the Hardy home and introduced himself as the owner of the Prescott stables. Frank and Joe thereupon told him of their interest in the *Topnotch* case and of finding the missing van.

The man was deeply interested.

"I may not have to pay that ransom after all!" he exclaimed. "Perhaps you young gentlemen would be good enough to take me to the place where you saw the truck?"

"Sure thing!" they both agreed.

They drove Mr. Prescott to the abandoned road, and then walked down the trail past the forbidding signs. They armed themselves with stout sticks in the event of an encounter with the dog, but their precautions were needless.

The animal did not appear, and they discovered the clearing without being molested.

A surprise awaited them. The boys gasped in disappointment.

"Why, the van is gone!" exclaimed Joe.

CHAPTER X

THE FOREIGNER'S HOUSE

Mr. Prescott glanced at his companions skeptically. He was wondering if the boys really had seen the truck. But their obvious dismay and bewilderment soon reassured him that they had.

"What could have happened to it?" wondered Frank.

"I suppose the thieves came and drove it away," replied Mr. Prescott. "Too bad we had to make this journey for nothing."

The Hardy boys were greatly chagrined, but the elderly gentleman made light of the matter. After all, he told them, it was the horse he wanted and not the van. He doubted that the vehicle would have given any clue as to the whereabouts of *Topnotch*.

"If you two lads would care to continue your investigation," he told them, "I should appreciate it very much. I don't mind telling you that I will gladly pay a reward of two thousand dollars for the return of my horse."

"We've started on this case and we don't

intend to give up now," they told him, with the assurance that they would do everything in their power to effect the return of the missing race-horse.

That evening the boys started discussing not only this mystery but also the strange affair of Vilnoff and the secret that lay behind his appearance on Barmet Bay at a time when Fenton Hardy presumably had left him in New York. It was Frank who offered a solution to this problem when he ventured the theory that perhaps the traveler had a brother who resembled him in appearance.

"We saw a man who looked like Vilnoff. Dad is positive he talked with Vilnoff in New York. The fellow couldn't be in two places at once; therefore, Vilnoff must have a double," reasoned Frank logically.

"What do you say to our going back to his house? We may be able to pick up some information."

"Isn't the place closed up?"

"No, I heard today that the servants are still in charge."

"Maybe we can persuade them to tell us something," said Frank.

One dim light was shining in a lower window of the Vilnoff residence when the boys arrived.

They ascended the front steps and rang the bell. At first there was no answer, but after some moments they heard footsteps in the hall. The door then swung open, and a butler appeared before them.

"Is Mr. Vilnoff at home?" inquired Frank. The man shook his head.

"I am sorry. Mr. Vilnoff sailed for Europe several days ago."

The boys pretended that this information came as a great surprise to them.

"When do you expect him back?"

"I'm sure I can't say, sir," replied the butler noncommittally.

"Then," said Joe, "may we speak to his brother, the other Mr. Vilnoff?"

The butler's face was impassive.

"Mr. Vilnoff has no brother, as far as I am aware, sir," he returned.

"I always thought he had a brother," said the Hardy boy.

"Indeed, sir? I am afraid you have been mistaken. No brother of Mr. Vilnoff has ever stayed here."

At this moment there came an interruption. From the lower part of the house there issued a sudden loud droning sound as if a motor had started up. This was followed immediately by a whirring noise.

The butler's face lost its look of studied impassivity. He was startled and evidently very much frightened.

"One moment, please!" he exclaimed hastily, and hurried down the hall, leaving the door wide open.

"Now's our chance!" whispered Frank, excited.

"What do you mean?"

"There's something queer about this place. I believe Vilnoff *is* here. Joe, you hide in the hall. When the butler comes back he'll think you have left. Then, later on, you can watch for a chance to let me in and we'll do some investigating."

The peculiar sounds of droning and whirring in the basement suddenly ceased.

"Hurry!" urged Frank.

Joe slipped across the threshold and glided into the hall. In the distance he could hear the sound of the butler's footsteps on the cellar stairs. Joe looked around for a hiding place, saw a heavy sofa in a room just off the hall, and dived behind it.

He was not a moment too soon. The servant appeared a few seconds later. He looked a little surprised when he found Frank waiting alone.

"Oh, the other boy is gone?" he said. Then, "I'm very sorry I cannot help you. But I am quite sure Mr. Vilnoff has no brother."

Frank pretended to be satisfied with the butler's statement.

"Very well," he answered. "I'm sorry if I have bothered you."

"Not at all, sir," replied the servant, and closed the door.

Frank went down the steps, conscious that the man was watching him through the glass in the door. Then he made his way along the front walk. As soon as he was out of sight of the veranda he ducked into the shrubbery. A few minutes later the porch light was extinguished, and he began creeping toward the house in the darkness.

He and Joe were running a big risk, it was clear to him. If they should be trapped this time they would not escape as lightly as they had on the previous occasion when the gardener and the chauffeur had caught them.

Frank eventually reached the big porch safely, and stole quietly up the steps. As he did so he saw a quick, sudden gleam of light at the window of the room in which Joe had hidden himself. For a moment the bright rays alarmed him. Then he realized that his brother had switched on his flashlight as a signal.

Frank moved silently across the veranda and waited at the entrance. He heard the knob rattle. Then the door swung open. At the same instant a bell in the house began ringing shrilly.

"Burglar alarm!" whispered Frank.

It had never occurred to the Hardy boys that the Vilnoff home might be protected in this manner. It was too late to back out now. Frank stepped inside and closed the door quickly. In the darkness Joe grabbed his arm.

"This way!" he whispered, and led Frank into the adjoining room. Joe had made good use of his time by sizing up the situation, and headed toward the heavy velvet curtains that hung before the front windows.

The bell was still ringing, and its jangling aroused the entire household. Frank and Joe could hear excited voices downstairs, followed by running footsteps. Someone came hurrying into the front hall and turned on the light. Another switch clicked, and the bell stopped ringing.

They heard a voice. It was answered by a second one. There were two men in the hall. The boys recognized one as that of the butler, but he was speaking in a foreign language. His companion answered in the same tongue.

Both servants then began a diligent search of the house. They entered the room in which the boys were hidden, and looked behind the sofa and chairs. One of them approached the window curtains, but just as he was about to draw them aside his companion called to him from the hall and the man withdrew. Frank and Joe, who had been breathless with suspense, were greatly relieved as they listened to his retreating footsteps.

The two lads experienced a bad ten minutes as the search continued, but finally the servants returned to the hall, examined the burglar alarm mechanism, and concluded that the contrivance must have gone off by accident. The pair held a long discussion in their own language, but finally went away, grumbling.

Frank and Joe remained hidden behind the curtains for some time. After a while they heard someone ascending the stairs at the rear of the house, and surmised that the butler was going to his own room. The place then became quiet.

"I guess we'd better clear out of here," whispered Joe. "We're lucky they didn't catch us."

"Now that we're in the house we might as well investigate that cellar again," returned Frank in guarded tones. "We may never have another chance."

Joe wasn't any too enthusiastic about the idea, but he offered no objections and followed his brother as he stole out from behind the drapes and moved quietly toward the hall. By the aid of Joe's flashlight they made their way into the kitchen. There the boys discovered a door that evidently led into the basement.

They opened it and went down the flight of steps.

The beam of the electric torch revealed the work-bench they had seen on the previous occasion when they had viewed the basement through the window. There seemed to be even more machinery in the place now. The stand was littered with scraps of metal and coils of wire. The boys became curious.

The light revealed a big electric motor and several heavy machines that they could not identify. Joe moved over to one of them and turned the light on it.

"I'd sure like to know what this place is for," he said in a puzzled tone. "I think our friend Vilnoff——"

As he took a step forward, a strange expression came over his face. He suddenly became rigid, then fell to the floor!

CHAPTER XI

Frank was horrified.

Had his brother been electrocuted? Had he stepped on some diabolical killing device in this underground chamber?

For a moment Frank Hardy was panic-stricken. His first impulse was to shout for help. Then his better judgment prevailed, and he knelt beside Joe, his finger on his brother's pulse.

Joe was alive, but evidently had been stunned by a powerful electric shock. By the gleam of his flashlight Frank saw a metal plate set in the floor. He dragged his brother away from it, loosened his collar and tie, and began rubbing his wrists in an effort to revive the stricken lad.

The shock had been severe. It was fully five minutes before Joe showed any signs of regaining consciousness. At length he sighed, opened his eyes, and muttered weakly:

"What happened?"

"You almost got yourself electrocuted," returned Frank in a relieved voice. "You put your foot on a charged metal plate and had a bad shock."

Joe managed to sit up, but he was very weak and still dazed by the powerful electric current that had knocked him senseless.

"Let's get out of here," he said.

The boys had lost all interest in any further exploration of the basement. Their sole desire now was to leave Vilnoff's house as quickly as possible. Frank helped Joe to his feet, but the lad was so dizzy that he could not stand up alone, much less walk unassisted.

Their plight was indeed dangerous. If their presence in the cellar should be discovered, Frank knew they would have no hope of escape because of Joe's uncertain condition. Then, too, if they were found in the house they would be unable to explain their presence to the angry servants.

"They would have us thrown in jail for house-breaking," Frank said to himself.

He managed to get Joe over to the basement steps. The task of reaching the kitchen above was far more difficult, and every moment Frank feared they would be heard. Luck was with them, however, and they got upstairs without arousing any members of the household. From the kitchen to the front door was the riskiest part of the journey. Supporting Joe with one arm, Frank tiptoed down the hall in the dark.

Then, sharp and clear, startling in the silence of the mysterious house, an electric bell shrilled. Frank's first thought was that it was another burglar alarm. On reflection, however, he identified the sound as the ringing of the door-bell.

Escape by the front way was now impossible. Already he could hear someone stirring above him preparing to answer the summons. From an upper hall there issued the sound of foot-steps.

Fortunately the corridor was in darkness. Frank hustled Joe into the room where they had taken refuge before, and once again the boys concealed themselves behind the velvet curtains. They were just in time. A second later the hall lights, which could be controlled by an upstairs switch, flashed on. Someone was coming down from the floor above.

It proved to be the butler. He proceeded gravely the length of the corridor and opened the door. Someone came into the house, saying:

"Where's Vilnoff?"

Frank thought the voice sounded familiar. At that moment, however, he could not remember when and where he had heard it before.

"Vilnoff isn't here," answered the butler shortly.

"Where is he?"

"On the ocean."

"On the ocean! What do you mean?"

"He sailed for Europe a couple of days ago."

The visitor was evidently surprised by this information.

"The quitter!" he snarled.

"Why do you wish to see him?" the servant inquired.

"It's about the signs. Who is going to take charge of 'em? They don't work, and I don't intend to get caught. Something's got to be done about 'em."

"I'll see that something is done," the butler assured him.

"You'd better. I'm not going to stand for any nonsense about those signs, I'm warning you."

"I'll send a message about it first thing tomorrow morning."

"See that you do!" growled the irate fellow. With that he stamped out onto the porch again, muttered "Goodnight," and went down the steps.

The butler closed the door, and Frank heard the click of a switch. This was followed at once by another similar sound, whereupon the hall lights went out. The servant returned to the stairs. Frank listened to his receding footsteps. Finally an upper door banged.

The problem of getting out by the front entrance without setting off the burglar alarm had been worrying Frank, but he thought he had solved the matter now. He had noticed that the alarm had not sounded when the butler admitted the stranger; nor had it rung when he and Joe called at the front entrance earlier in the evening.

Clearly, then, the signal could be switched on and off as desired. He recalled that the servant had paused a moment in the hallway before opening the door to the visitor. Then he had heard the click of some switch before the light switch was thrown off.

Frank helped Joe into the hall. With his flashlight he scanned the row of push-buttons beside the door. Over each of them, with one exception, was a tiny card indicating the lights it controlled, such as "Lower Hall," "Upper Hall," "Library," and "Living Room." The unmarked button was set a little aside from the others.

"If this isn't the burglar alarm control, we'll be in plenty of trouble," Frank whispered to Joe, as he moved the switch. Then, turning the door handle, he prepared for immediate flight.

But there was no clamorous bell to alarm the household. The door opened silently and easily. In another moment the boys were out on the porch and Frank was turning the knob behind them.

Joe was so weak that he could scarcely walk,

so their progress was necessarily slow. But they gained the darkness of the driveway in safety and from there escape was easy. In a few minutes the Hardy boys were out on the sidewalk, homeward bound.

Under a corner street lamp they stopped to rest, for Joe was so shaken and exhausted that he was on the verge of collapse. He was still suffering from the effects of the electric shock.

"I'll be O.K. after a while," he told Frank, "but I still feel sick and dizzy."

The fresh air appeared to revive him somewhat, and after a short rest the lad felt well enough to proceed. At that moment a car that had been speeding down the road ground to a sudden stop, and a familiar voice shouted:

"Hi! Come on for a ride!"

It was Chet Morton, accompanied by his cousin Bill.

"You couldn't have turned up at a better time," declared Frank as he and his brother walked over to the auto. "I'm just trying to get Joe home. He's not feeling very well."

"What's the matter? Gosh, you *do* look sick!" exclaimed Chet, noticing his friend's white face. "Been sampling one of your Dad's cigars, by any chance?"

"He suffered an electric shock," explained Frank as he helped Joe into the car.

"How come?"

"Oh, we were doing a little sleuthing," Frank answered evasively. "We got into a place where we had no right to be, and Joe suffered for it."

"Lucky I wasn't killed," Joe said feebly.

"I'd like to hear about it. Did it have anything to do with this *Topnotch* affair?" asked Chet.

"No. Something else. We'll tell you all about it another time."

"I think you fellows ought to entertain Bill with a little sleuthing while he's visiting here," declared Chet, as he drove the car toward the Hardy home.

"Gee, I wish you would!" exclaimed his cousin. "Is detective work very dangerous?"

"Well, you see what happened to Joe," observed Chet. "Came within an inch of being fried."

"You and Bill might come out with us on that *Topnotch* case, if you care to," said Frank. "We picked up some clues in that affair and we hope to locate the race-horse."

"It's a go!" Chet declared promptly. "How about it, Bill?"

"Sure, I'm game for anything," answered his cousin.

They had reached the Hardy place by this time, and Frank suggested that they all go in for a bite to eat.

"Not a word about that electric shock to anyone," cautioned Joe, who was feeling a little
better. "If Dad, or Mother, or Aunt Gertrude
should get wise to it they'd turn thumbs down
on any more detective work for us."

The others agreed not to mention Joe's mis-
hap, as they all went up to the house. When
they entered the hall they found Mrs. Hardy
at the telephone.

"No, I'm sorry, they're not in," she was saying. Then, as the door opened and she turned
and saw the boys, she cried, "Oh, just a moment, please. Frank and Joe are coming
in now."

She handed the former lad the receiver.
"Someone calling you," she whispered.

"Hello. This is Frank Hardy."

"Mr. Prescott speaking," said a trembling
voice. "You remember me. I'm the owner of
Topnotch."

"Yes, Mr. Prescott. Any news?"

"Bad news," replied the other.

CHAPTER XII

"Bad news?" repeated Frank. "What has happened, Mr. Prescott?"

"I can't tell you over the telephone. Do you mind if I drop in for a few minutes? I'd like to see your father."

"Dad isn't in town just now. But you're welcome to come over anyway."

"Fine. I'll be there within half an hour."

Frank turned away from the telephone. He wondered what had happened to prompt this unexpected call from the owner of *Topnotch*.

"All right, you fellows," he said to Chet and Bill. "Now is your chance to get a taste of a real live mystery. We'll let you sit in on our little chat with Mr. Prescott."

Mrs. Hardy prepared sandwiches and cocoa for the boys. While they were enjoying this light repast Frank and Joe explained the *Topnotch* case to the extent of their own knowledge of the affair. Chet and Bill, therefore, knew all the essential facts in the affair by the time Mr. Prescott finally arrived.

The man from Kentucky looked worried and anxious. "When will your father be back?" he asked abruptly. "I want him to take this case."

"Dad has been pretty busy," replied Frank. "He may not return tonight at all. Perhaps you'd like to tell us what has happened."

The gentleman sank into a comfortable arm-chair.

"All that has occurred," he said heavily, "is that I've been swindled out of twenty-five thousand dollars."

"You paid the ransom!" cried Joe.

"Yes, I paid it, but I didn't get *Topnotch* back."

The boys were shocked. It was bad enough to pay a huge ransom for the stolen race-horse, but to lose the animal after acceding to the kidnapers' demands was a real tragedy.

"They sent me letters," explained Mr. Prescott. "They proved to me that they actually had *Topnotch* in their possession by mentioning a certain hidden mark on his body. I left the money at a place we agreed upon and the horse was to have been sent to the Spurtown track stables by truck. But the crooks double-crossed me. Your father will have to take this case for me."

"My brother and I could fill in until Dad comes home," offered Frank.

Mr. Prescott looked dubious.

"I appreciate your help, of course," he said politely, "but after all this case is one for a real detective such as Fenton Hardy. A great deal of money is involved, you realize."

Chet broke in at this moment. "I guess you don't understand, Mr. Prescott," he said. "The Hardy boys are real detectives. They aren't professionals, perhaps, but they have solved plenty of mysteries that specialists have failed in."

Chet loyally went on to tell the caller about some of the sensational cases which the Hardy boys had handled. The horse owner was surprised and interested. His manner altered at once.

"Well, then, until your father returns you may substitute for him," he said. It was evident, however, that Mr. Prescott hoped Fenton Hardy would soon be back and take the case into his own hands.

After the man had left the house the boys discussed the *Topnotch* affair and agreed that they should get busy as soon as possible. Bill and Chet were enthusiastic over the prospect of assisting, and agreed to be back at the Hardy home early next morning to spend the whole day searching for the stolen race-horse.

"Bring some lunch along and a couple of flashlights," advised Frank. "We may be away until dark."

"Where are we going?" asked Chet's cousin.

"You'll know when we get there," laughed Joe. "Be prepared to do plenty of walking."

It was the Hardy boys' intention to go back to the clearing where they had seen the van and make a thorough investigation, in the hope of picking up some further clue that might help them to trace the crooks.

Next morning, however, the boys were unable to start out as early as they had planned. A telegram arrived from Fenton Hardy asking them to remain at the house to receive a message from a client who would be driving through Bayport during the afternoon. It was important that they receive the man personally, so the boys were obliged to wait. It was not until after three o'clock that he called and left some papers for a case Mr. Hardy was handling.

Chet and Bill had been waiting out on the back porch for more than an hour before Joe and Frank were finally free. Then, with their sandwiches, flashlights and compasses they all piled into Chet's car and set out in the direction of Spurtown.

At the crossroads the stout lad was instructed to turn to the right. They proceeded along the abandoned road as far as they could, then got out of the car and went on foot. They passed the sign that advised trespassers to "keep out," and followed the winding trail until they reached the place where the dog had chased Frank and Joe into the woods.

The animal did not appear. The four lads walked down the trail unmolested. At length Frank spied wheel marks in the ground.

"These must have been left by the van when they moved it," he said, as the boys made their way to the clearing.

This time they searched every inch of the ground very thoroughly, but without finding anything in the nature of a clue.

"Strikes me that this detective business is just a lot of plain, ordinary hard work," remarked Bill Morton.

"You asked for it," replied his cousin unsympathetically.

The boys left the clearing and picked up another trail that led still deeper into the woods. This one was wide enough to permit passage of a truck. Although they examined the ground carefully, they could find no wheel marks or any evidence that such a vehicle had passed that way.

"The ground is hard and plenty of leaves have fallen during the past few days," said Joe. "Even though we can't find any tracks, I have a hunch that the van came this way after it was driven out of the clearing."

Suddenly Frank stopped, a puzzled expression on his face.

"That tree, Joe!" he exclaimed, pointing to

a bare, leafless oak some distance ahead. "I saw its branches move."

"What of it?" demanded Chet's cousin.

"There isn't any wind."

"Gosh, I never thought of that. Then what is it that makes the branches move?"

"That's what puzzles me," returned Frank.

"It's a queer-looking tree, too," remarked Joe. "All the boughs grow in the same direction."

Joe and Frank advanced carefully. The closer they came to the odd looking growth the more unnatural it appeared. Once again they were sure they saw a movement in the stiff, bare branches.

On close inspection they received a distinct surprise. The tree was artificial!

The branches were merely wired to the trunk, and the whole object appeared to be set in an iron base partly covered with dead leaves.

"Now what do you make of that?" exclaimed Joe, profoundly astonished.

"I guess those branches did move after all," Frank said. "They must be some sort of a signal. That's why they all point in the same direction."

"If it's a signal, how is it worked?"

"Mechanically, I suppose. It has certainly been put here for some purpose."

Chet and his cousin came up at this moment.

When they learned about the artificial oak, Bill Morton began to look nervous.

"I—I don't think we ought to fool around here any longer," he quavered. "Let's go on home."

"Just when things are beginning to get interesting? Not me," rejoined Chet.

Frank and Joe were very curious about the strange tree. They did not doubt but that it was a signal of some kind. However, they could not discover what made it move. They walked back and forth and jumped on the ground near the strange growth, but nothing happened.

"Queer!" said Frank. "There may be other trees like it somewhere a little ways ahead. Let's go on."

They went forward through the woods, following the trail all the while, but found no more artificial trees. Before they had traversed more than a few hundred yards, however, their progress was suddenly thwarted. A high barrier of barbed wire rose before them.

"A fence in a forest!" exclaimed Joe. "I wonder what's the reason for that?"

They could not go ahead, so they made their way along the barbed wire enclosure in the belief that it did not extend very far. Soon they came to a sign hanging from the top strand. It emphatically warned trespassers away from the place.

PRIVATE KENNELS

Vicious Dogs at Large

KEEP OUT!

Frank and Joe looked at each other.

"I don't believe it!" declared the latter.

"You don't believe that sign?" exclaimed Bill Morton. "Why, it says in black and white that there are vicious dogs inside. You couldn't get me to go in there for anything."

"I think it's a hoax. What do you say, Frank? Are you game to climb that fence with me?"

"Sure. Chet and Bill can stay here and keep watch."

Frank made this suggestion because he knew that Chet's cousin had no desire whatsoever to test the authenticity of the sign. Then, too, Chet himself was not very enthusiastic about climbing the fence.

"O.K.," said Joe Hardy without further delay, hunting out the nearest post.

He then began to scale the strands of wire, clambered over the fence without getting caught on the barbs and dropped to the ground. Frank followed, and in a few moments the two boys had disappeared into the gloom of the trees.

"If this is detective work," said Bill Morton,

looking around apprehensively, "then I'd rather be back in school."

Chet waited with his cousin in the gathering twilight. He was restless, and suggested that they might as well investigate the fence a little while the Hardy boys were absent. The two lads followed it for a short distance through the woods. Then the trees thinned out.

"Why, I see a gate!" exclaimed the fat boy.

The barbed wires were broken by a stout wooden gate, chained and padlocked. A road led up to it through the woods and wound off among the trees inside. On the gate-post was a sign similar to the one the boys had seen on the fence.

Chet sauntered over to examine the padlock and chain. Timidly his cousin followed.

"Do you hear anything?" asked Bill, looking around.

Chet listened. In the distance the boys could hear a steady throbbing and humming.

"It's a car of some kind," remarked Chet. Then, as the sound became steadily louder, he said, "By golly, it's coming this way!"

"Oh, gosh!" quavered Bill. "We'll both be captured!"

There was no doubt but that a truck was lumbering through the woods, rattling along the trail by which they had come at a good rate of speed. Chet wasted no time. He flung himself on the ground and began heaping dead leaves over himself.

"Hurry!" he urged his cousin. "Cover up and they'll never see us."

Bill did not have to be coaxed. Frantically he began burrowing among the leaves, and in a few minutes there was nothing but a pair of mounds to indicate the presence of the two boys.

The truck lurched unsteadily and came to a halt at the gate. Chet and Bill heard someone unfasten the padlock. The chain rattled. The machine passed through. A moment later the gate was closed and secured again. Then the lumbering contraption rumbled away inside the enclosure.

In a few minutes Chet sat up, brushing the leaves aside.

"I hope Frank and Joe don't run into any trouble—" he began.

Then his heart began to pound. From out of the depths of the woods on the other side of the fence he heard a long-drawn, heart-rending scream!

CHAPTER XIII

THE CABIN IN THE WOODS

In the meantime Frank and Joe Hardy made a discovery. They had proceeded through the woods for about two hundred yards when they came upon an open place. In the middle of it stood a large cabin. Dusk had now descended, and the boys had little fear of being seen as they crouched beneath the trees on the outskirts of the tiny clearing.

"I think the cabin is empty," said Joe. "Let's go and make sure."

Frank was more cautious, however. "We'll wait a few minutes," he said.

The boys were glad that they delayed. A moment later a light sprang up in one of the cabin windows, and against the glare a figure suddenly appeared. They could see the man only in silhouette, but both boys gave an involuntary gasp of surprise.

"Vilnoff!" whispered Joe excitedly.

The black shadow against the window blind was very much like that of Vilnoff. As they watched, they saw the man's arm raised. In his hand he held an object that resembled another hand.

"Just like the model we found beside Vilnoff's house," Frank whispered.

The boys crept across the clearing until they got closer to the cabin. They could now hear voices from within the building. Crouching beneath the window, they listened closely but could hear no sound. They did, however, smell the odor of food cooking.

Suddenly a man's voice said, "I'll take their supper up to 'em."

Then there came a clattering of dishes and the sound of footsteps as if someone were ascending a flight of stairs. The boys had noticed a window in the upper part of the cabin. A light suddenly appeared from it.

"How long is I got to stay heah, boss?" grumbled a plaintive voice. "Doggone if I wants to be cooped up in dis place much longer."

It was the voice of a Negro.

The Hardy boys immediately thought of the colored man who had been with the horse van on the road to Spurtown. Was he being kept a prisoner in this remote place?

"I'm going to climb up there and have a look," whispered Frank.

"Careful," warned his brother. "If we're caught now it will spoil everything."

The logs at the end of the cabin afforded a

precarious foothold, and Frank began making his way up toward the window. Once he almost fell, but recovered himself in time and managed to grab at a jutting log. From there he swung himself over to the window-sill, and peered through the glass.

What met his eyes was an attic room, sparsely furnished with two cots, a small table, and some empty boxes. On one of the small beds some-one lay sleeping.

Two men were standing beside a table. One of them was colored; the other, who was just putting down a supper tray, was white. Frank had never seen him before but he thought he recognized the Negro as the driver of the van.

"Ah wants to go home," he was saying. "I'se gettin' tired of stayin' in dis yeah place."

"But your boss doesn't want yuh yet," the other man objected. "No use goin' back until he sends for yuh."

"Ah wants to get back t' mah horses," wailed the Negro. "No fun settin' aroun' heah day after day. Cain't understan' why mah boss don't want me."

Frank was so excited that he raised his head well above the level of the sill to get a better view of the interior of the attic room.

"Well, you're going to stay here and that's all there is to it," said the white stranger. "What are yuh kickin' about? You've got a place to sleep and enough to eat, haven't yuh?''

"Ah doan' believe mah boss knows about me bein' heah at all," returned the Negro suspiciously.

"Mean to say I've been lying to yuh?"

The stableman nodded.

"Ah is gwine get out of heah and get to de race-track, dat's what Ah is gwine do," he announced. He made a step toward the head of the stairway, but the other fellow quickly barred his way.

"No, you don't!" he growled. "You're not leavin' this cabin, see!"

The colored man was powerfully built. He brushed his white antagonist aside and sent him staggering. Instantly there was a fight in progress, the attendant trying to restrain his prisoner from reaching the head of the stairs.

Frank was highly excited. He was oblivious to the fact that his shadow against the lighted window would be visible to anyone approaching the cabin.

Joe, on the other hand, was vainly trying to attract his brother's attention. For several moments he had heard the distant rumble of an approaching machine. It appeared to be coming through the woods in the direction of the clearing.

He could not call out to attract Frank's attention, for he realized there was another man downstairs in the cabin. Several times the silhouette of the individual resembling Vilnoff had appeared at the window.

The truck was now close at hand. Joe saw the headlights swing toward the clearing. He did not know what to do. Frank was completely absorbed by the fight going on in the attic, his head and shoulders plainly visible above the window sill.

The beam of the truck's headlights fell directly on him. There was a yell from the driver.

Frank turned suddenly, saw first the vehicle, then his brother gesturing frantically below. He ducked beneath the level of the window sill. At the same time one of his feet slipped and he lost his balance. He grabbed wildly at the sill for support, but missed.

"Oh gee!" gasped Joe.

At that moment there was a terrified scream.

CHAPTER XIV

DID VILNOFF SAIL?

When Bill Morton heard that terrible scream from the heart of the woods he uttered a low groan.

"Somebody's being murdered!" he said in a quavering voice to his cousin. "I wish I were home."

"I'd kinda like to be somewhere else myself," remarked Chet, sitting up among the leaves. "Gosh, I hope nothing has happened to Frank and Joe."

"We'll never see them alive!" predicted Bill dolefully.

"They've been in some pretty tight places before this and they've always managed to wriggle through," said Chet, but he was nervous. "I—I suppose it's our duty to go and see what has happened——"

Bill Morton positively quaked at this suggestion. "What good would that do?" he demanded. "If they've been slaughtered in cold blood we couldn't help them now."

Chet and his cousin were in a dilemma. They

were none too enthusiastic about climbing the gate and going up the road to investigate.

"Maybe we'd better wait a little while. Then, if they don't show up, we can go and get help," decided Chet.

In about ten minutes they heard the rumble of the truck again. They crouched down beside the road well out of range of the advancing head-lights.

The van halted. The driver got out, unlocked the gate and drove the machine through. Again he got out, this time to fasten the iron gates. Then he returned to his seat at the wheel and started the truck going.

During the delay Chet had noticed something moving in the back of the van. Just as the driver resumed his place the stout lad saw that two figures were in the rear, gesturing to him.

"The Hardys!" he cried.

So relieved was he that he forgot the need of caution. Fortunately the noise of the engine drowned out his involuntary shout, otherwise the man at the wheel would have heard him.

The huge vehicle was slowly moving away from the gate when Chet and Bill scrambled hastily out of the ditch and gave chase. The latter made a flying leap and hauled himself up into the van. Chet, fat and pudgy, would have had a difficult time getting inside, had not his friends reached out, grabbed him by the shirt and the slack of the trousers, and hauled him in.

Frank then closed the doors at the back and put his fingers across his lips for silence. As they did not dare to be overheard by the driver, they sat still while the machine jolted down the rough road through the woods.

Finally the going became easier and the truck bowled along at a good rate of speed. The boys did not know in what direction they were being taken, but Frank felt convinced that they were now out on the Spurtown road. Whether they were bound for that place or Bayport he was unable to make out.

At length the vehicle came to a stop. The boys heard the driver step down. Frank opened the door a trifle and peered out.

"This is luck," he thought.

A short distance away he could see a service station and lunch room. The place looked familiar to him. Then he recognized it as the one where he and Joe had encountered Gus and his friend Pete, the truck-driver.

"This is great," he told his companions. "We're out on the Bayport road now, and can catch a bus for home. Let's get away from here."

He watched closely as the driver went into the service station. Beyond the window he could see the burly form of Gus, the proprietor. He and the other fellow disappeared into the rear of the establishment, so Frank hastily flung open the doors of the truck and the boys scrambled out.

They lost no time gaining the shelter of the darkness beyond the range of the service station's lights. Joe looked at his watch and saw that they would have to wait about ten minutes for a bus, so they decided to walk slowly to its next stopping place.

"We thought something terrible had happened," confessed Chet. "Who let out that awful yell? If you hadn't shown up we were going to set out for help."

"We were nearly caught," Joe said.

He and Frank told their companions about their discovery of the cabin in the clearing, and related how they had seen the shadow of someone who resembled Vilnoff. Frank informed them of the incident at the attic window.

"I'm sure the Negro saw my face," he said. "He was the one who screamed. Maybe because he saw me, maybe because the other fellow knocked him down. I don't know."

"What happened then?" asked Bill, wild-eyed.

"When the headlights of the truck were turned on me, I was blinded for an instant," replied Frank.

"Then he saw me waving my arms up and down," went on Joe. "I hadn't dared yell, for

Vilnoff or whoever it was would have come out.''

"Go on," prodded Chet, as the Hardys paused.

"I lost my balance," said Frank. "I grabbed for the sill, missed it, and——"

"Fell to the ground," finished Joe. "Scared me to death. But when I rushed over to Frank, he was all right. I helped him up, and we ran."

"We just got out of sight when the truck reached the cabin and stopped. Then someone came running through the woods."

"We were hiding behind some bushes and heard the driver tell the other man about Frank," explained his brother. "They started a search, so we were in a tight spot."

"Then you hid in the truck," laughed Chet. "Bright boys. Well, thanks for getting us safely away from that place."

"You bet," chimed in Bill. "And I've had enough detective work!"

"The driver couldn't figure out where Frank had gone, for he was pretty sure he had seen someone when the headlights swung past the cabin," Joe added. "Of course, the moment we saw our chance we climbed into the back of the truck. That was the last place they would ever think of searching. Finally they gave up and went into the building. One of them came out a few minutes later and drove away."

"It was lucky you fellows stayed near the gate," Frank remarked. "As it was, we all saved ourselves a long walk."

"Well, this sort of fun may be all right for some people," said Bill Morton, "but I can't see it. I'm through with sleuthing. You walk for miles, you get half scared to death, you endure a bumpy ride in the back of a truck, you walk a couple of miles more in the dark, miss your supper, and come home on a bus."

"A little strenuous for you, Bill?" asked Joe.

"I guess I'm not cut out to be a detective, that's all," returned Chet's cousin good-humoredly. "As far as I'm concerned, that race-horse can stay lost."

When Frank and Joe reached home that night they received the customary reprimand from Aunt Gertrude because they were late to dinner. It disappointed them to learn that Fenton Hardy had not yet returned home. However, their mother had received a telegram that afternoon.

"Home tomorrow. Want boys to be there."

"Too bad Dad isn't here tonight," said Frank. "I have a few hunches I'd like to talk over with him."

"This affair seems to be getting more complicated each day," returned Joe. "For instance, do you think that was Vilnoff in the cabin tonight?"

"We saw only his shadow, but it looked mighty like him."

"And you say the colored fellow upstairs resembled the driver of the horse van?"

"Yes."

"Then maybe there's a connection. I feel Vilnoff may be mixed up in some shady business at that house of his, but I never dreamed that he could be connected with the *Topnotch* affair, did you?"

"It doesn't sound reasonable," admitted Frank, "that a man as wealthy as Vilnoff is said to be would stoop to horse-thieving."

"And what is the idea behind that strange mechanical tree? I can't figure that one out at all," said Joe.

"Why is the Negro being kept a prisoner in the cabin? That's another one for you."

"Where is *Topnotch?* And who has the ransom money?"

"There are so many whys in this case that I'm getting muddled," said Frank. "Maybe we can think more clearly when we've had a good night's sleep."

Fenton Hardy returned home early next morning. He was in the dining room when the boys came down to breakfast. The great detective greeted his sons affably but appeared thoughtful and preoccupied. When they told him about Mr. Prescott's visit and the racing man's request that Mr. Hardy take the *Top-notch* case, their father had little to say.

"We'll talk about that later," he remarked quietly. "In the meantime I have something to show you. Come into the library after you have eaten your breakfast."

When they got there they found their father setting up a small home movie projection machine. On the table lay a circular tin of motion picture film.

"I picked this up at the Quickshot office in New York yesterday," Fenton Hardy explained. "They followed your instructions and took movies of all the passengers that sailed on the *Atlantis*. I didn't have time to look at them yesterday but we'll run the film through now."

He pinned a white sheet to the wall, threaded the strips into the machine, drew the shades and snapped a switch. The motor of the projection machine began to hum and a bright square of light flashed onto the screen. Then the boys found themselves looking at the gangplank of the *Atlantis*, which the passengers were ascending to board the ship.

For about five minutes the film showed a steady procession of people. The pictures were very clear, and as the men and women walked up in single file not one of them had escaped the sharp eye of the camera.

Suddenly from the side of the screen the familiar figure of a man emerged. He strode up the gangplank, and in doing so evidently became aware of the camera, for he suddenly looked around and faced the machine. He said something, probably to the cameraman, and abruptly turned away, ducking his head and hurrying into the ship.

"Vilnoff!" exclaimed Frank.

"Looks like him, doesn't it?" remarked Mr. Hardy.

"Then we're wrong about his being at the cabin last night," murmured Joe.

Fenton Hardy stopped the camera, ran the film back, then started it going again. Once more they saw the familiar figure rush up the gangplank, turn, gaze at the machine, and hurry into the ship.

"We may as well be sure," said the boys' father.

He ran the film through several times, and at each showing the three watchers studied the screen intently.

"It looks like Vilnoff, all right," declared Frank slowly. "And yet it seems to me that there is something different."

"Queer," said Joe. "I have the same idea, too. What can it be?"

Fenton Hardy ran the reel through the machine once again. This time Frank gave a sudden shout.

"Now I know!" he cried.   "Why didn't I think of that before?"

"What's the matter?" asked Joe.

"I'm sure Vilnoff didn't sail on the *Atlantis!* That man must be his double."

CHAPTER XV

"WHAT makes you so sure the man on the screen is not Vilnoff?" asked Mr. Hardy. "He certainly resembles him very closely."

"When we met Vilnoff at his house one night I noticed he had a peculiar mannerism," said Frank. "I saw it the afternoon he sat beside me at the football game, too. Whenever he spoke he would blink a lot. He also had a habit of holding up his right hand, opening and closing it nervously. The man on the screen isn't doing that."

"He's carrying a bag," objected Joe, "so how could he hold up his hand?"

"Yes, but he is holding it in his left hand. His right arm is free. You notice he has evidently said something to the cameraman or to somebody near by and didn't even move his right arm when he spoke."

Fenton Hardy was interested.

"We'll run that film through once more," he said. "You may be right at that, Frank."

Again the picture flickered on the white

123

screen, and the man who looked like **Vilnoff** came up the gangplank carrying a bag.

"You're right," admitted Joe. "He has it in his left hand."

They watched closely as the fellow turned, saw the camera, spoke, wheeled away and hurried into the ship. His right hand had not moved, nor had he blinked.

"Very good observation, Frank," said Fenton Hardy approvingly. "I guess you are right in thinking that Vilnoff has a double."

"The man who boarded the *Atlantis* must have been the one who took the plane from Bayport that morning. That's why he didn't recognize us when he passed the *Sleuth* out in the bay."

"Can't you send a radiogram to the ship and have the fellow held when the *Atlantis* reaches port?" asked Joe.

Fenton Hardy shook his head.

"We have no proof as to his identity. We would have to find the real Vilnoff before we could prove that the other fellow is his double, if such a person exists. That's your problem now. Find the real Vilnoff."

Fenton Hardy had to be a witness in a court case that morning so the boys were left to their own resources. They told their father something of their activities in the *Topnotch* affair, but Mr. Hardy said he was so busy with other matters that he would be unable to do anything in the case of the missing race-horse just then. He advised his sons to follow up their own investigations.

"If I can get in touch with Mr. Prescott," said the detective, "I'll explain the situation to him and advise him to leave it in your hands for the present. You seem to have done very well without my help. In the meantime, I wish you would try to learn where Vilnoff is keeping himself."

"You're not going to tell us yet why you want him?" asked Frank.

The detective smiled. "Professional secret, my boy. But the man must be located."

After Fenton Hardy left the house on his way to court, the boys happened to pick up the morning paper. On one of the sports pages they found an item that interested them. It was headed:

JOCKEY IVAN TO RIDE
PRESCOTT STABLE ENTRY

The article stated that the Kentucky stables had secretly shipped one of its finest horses to a city in an adjacent state, where a race was to be held during the following week.

"Mr. Prescott is taking no more chances on

losing a valuable horse—hence the secrecy in shipping the animal," the story ran. "No further trace of *Topnotch,* star performer of the Prescott stables, has been found since the animal disappeared while being transported to the Spurtown meet. Jockey Ivan, who has been there this week, will leave tonight, and has high hopes of riding the Prescott stable entry to victory in next week's race."

This news aroused the Hardy boys at once. If they expected to get any further information from Jockey Ivan they realized that they would have to see him before he should leave the state.

"We'd better drive over to Spurtown and look him up," said Frank.

The boys got into their roadster and drove over at once. At the race-track they sought news of the young rider, but learned that he had not been seen around the stables that morning. A friendly trainer, however, gave them Ivan's address, which was a lodging house not far away.

The landlady, an elderly, capable-looking woman, regarded her callers shrewdly.

"I'll see if he's in," she said, and went puffing up the stairs. A moment later she called down from the landing, "Ye can come up. He says he'll see ye."

Ivan was just packing his trunk.

"Hello, fellows!" he said cheerfully. "I'm

glad to see you. Just getting ready to pull out of town.''

"The newspaper account said you wouldn't be going until tonight,'' said Frank.

"I changed my mind. I'm leaving by an earlier train. Well, what's new? Any more information about *Topnotch?*''

Frank shrugged. "We haven't made much progress," he admitted. "We came over to ask you a question.''

"Fire ahead!'' invited the jockey. "Glad to give you any help I can.''

"You were talking to a man by the name of Vilnoff at the track the other day. It was the afternoon the automobile broke loose, if you remember.''

A shadow seemed to flit over the jockey's face when Frank mentioned Vilnoff's name.

"Yes?''

"He's a friend of yours, isn't he? What do you know about him?''

Jockey Ivan did not seem disposed to answer any questions about the fellow, and became evasive. A suspicion meanwhile had been forming in Frank's mind. If Vilnoff was involved in the theft of the race-horse, perhaps Jockey Ivan was mixed up in the affair as well, since he and Vilnoff were friends.

"I know him, yes. Can't tell you much about him. Lives in Bayport, I believe,'' offered Ivan, and stopped. This was all they could get out of him on the subject of the man.

"What would you say if we were to tell you that he stole *Topnotch?*" asked Joe suddenly.

The jockey looked at them strangely. Then he flushed.

"I'd say it was a lie," he answered quickly.

Ivan seemed positive in this opinion. Before the boys could question him further, they heard the doorbell ring. Then the landlady came panting up the stairs once more.

"There's some gentlemen here to take ye to the station, Mr. Ivan," she said, fanning herself with her apron. "From the Racin' Association, they say they be. Waitin' out there in a fine big car."

"From the Racing Association!" exclaimed the jockey. "That's swell. I'll be right down, Mrs. Clancy."

"My poor husband—may he rest in peace," said the woman, "was one of the finest jockeys that ever booted a three-year-old under the wire, but never did he have people from the Racin' Association comin' around to take him for a drive. Ye're a lucky boy, Mr. Ivan, to have those grand people showin' such an interest in ye."

She left the room, still fanning herself. Ivan closed his trunk and locked it.

Shaking hands with the Hardy boys, he said,

"I'm sorry I have to rush away like this, but maybe we'll see each other again."

"Let's hope so," returned Frank.

They went downstairs with the jockey, who said good-bye to his landlady. Then the three stepped outside.

A big closed car was standing at the curb. As Ivan entered it, Frank and Joe caught a glimpse of a man huddled in the back seat. He attracted their attention because of a black patch that covered one of his eyes. The boys did not have a chance to observe the other occupants, for as soon as the door closed behind the jockey the auto pulled ahead and shot swiftly out of sight around the corner.

"Frank!" exclaimed Joe excitedly, "did you get a good view of that man with the patch over his eye?"

"I couldn't see him very clearly," Frank admitted.

"I could. And he was Vilnoff!"

Frank was startled.

"Are you sure?"

"Positive."

"Then let us hustle down to the railway station at once."

The Hardy boys jumped into their roadster and drove to the corner. The other car was not in sight, so they asked directions to the railroad station. In a few minutes they reached

it, jumped out, and hurried down the plat-
form.

Of Jockey Ivan and Vilnoff they could find no
trace. The car that had called at the rider's
lodging house was not in evidence anywhere.

When the train arrived ten minutes later and
Ivan still had failed to appear, the boys were
puzzled. All their inquiries were fruitless.

"The landlady distinctly said that the men
from the Racing Association were waiting to
drive him to the station!" declared Joe.

"I'm sure Vilnoff doesn't belong to any
Racing Association!" said Frank. "There's
something queer about this affair. I hope Ivan
hasn't stepped into a trap. He's a nice fellow."

"Yes," agreed his brother. "But he seemed
to know more about Vilnoff than he cared to
tell!"

The Hardy boys questioned several people in
Spurtown that afternoon, even going back to
the jockey's lodging house. The landlady said
the young man's trunk had been picked up
shortly before train-time. She had heard nothing from him since his departure.

Finally they put in a long distance call to the
racing stables where Ivan was to have reported
that afternoon. The replies to their inquiries
only served to deepen the mystery.

"Jockey Ivan?" said the official who answered the telephone. "No, he hasn't arrived

here; in fact, we've received word that he has changed his mind and isn't going to come after all."

"Did Ivan himself give you that message?"

"No, someone telephoned and told us."

Frank was greatly perplexed. Even though Vilnoff might be back of some underhanded schemes, the Hardy boy was almost certain that the jockey had no part in them. But it began to look as if the two had something to do with the disappearance of *Topnotch*.

"By the way," he asked the landlady, "what is Ivan's last name?"

"Why, it's Evans," she answered. "But I always call him Mr. Ivan."

The boys left the lodging house and drove toward Bayport, still discussing the day's events.

"Ivan is a foreign name," commented Frank. "Do you suppose Evans is an assumed American one?"

"Don't know," replied Joe. "What I do know is that I like the fellow, and I don't like Vilnoff. And so——"

"Yes?"

"I believe Ivan's honest. What's more, I think he's been kidnaped!"

"I'm inclined to agree with you, Joe. It's up to us to rescue him!"

CHAPTER XVI

THE UNDERGROUND PASSAGE

When the boys returned to their home in Bayport that night they had formulated a new plan. Vilnoff, they believed, was lurking somewhere behind the strange series of events that had resulted in the theft of the race-horse and the disappearance of Ivan Evans.

The strange foreigner, they felt, could reveal the name of the man who had sailed on the *Atlantis*. That mystery, and everything else, centred around the eccentric Vilnoff.

"We'll go straight to headquarters for our information," declared Frank. "We'll make another search of the fellow's house."

They realized fully the danger they were likely to run into. To offset any worry on the part of their father, they left a note for him with instructions to send the police to the Vilnoff place as well as to the cabin in the woods, should the boys fail to return home by midnight. Frank sketched a map giving complete directions for reaching the shack.

They set out after dark and made their approach to the Vilnoff house very cautiously. For several minutes they stood outside the fence, watching the place until they were convinced that no one was lurking in the grounds.

"We must learn more about what's going on in that cellar," Frank decided. "And we just can't afford to be caught prowling around, either."

They crossed the lawn safely, flitting from tree to tree and from bush to bush until at last they were in the deep shadows at one side of the house.

"The cellar light is on," whispered Joe.

They could see the yellow rectangle of illumination beyond a clump of barberry. Quietly they crept forward to the window.

Here they met with a disappointment. The casement had been covered on the inside with a coating of cream colored paint. Nothing of the basement beyond was visible.

For a while the boys crouched, listening intently. They could hear a constant whirr of machinery and an occasional clank-clank of metal on metal, followed by the rending noise of a saw cutting through iron. Once in a while someone coughed, then walked around.

Frank tried the side of the window. It was loose.

"Maybe I can move it out enough to see what is going on in there," he whispered.

He again tugged gently at the side of the casement and it gave slightly. Another tug, and the window slipped in Frank's grasp. To his horror, one elbow crashed completely through the glass.

The shattering of the pane made a tremendous racket in the stillness of the night. To make matters worse, the frame slipped through Frank's fingers, causing the whole sash to tumble into the cellar. It fell on the concrete floor of the basement with a splintering crash.

Through the opening the boys could see someone run across the floor of the basement to a door at the back of the room. They recognized the figure immediately.

The man was Vilnoff!

For an instant the man's face was clearly revealed to them in the electric light. Then he pulled open the door and vanished.

"After him!"

Frank was scrambling through the open window. He dropped onto the concrete floor and rushed in pursuit. Joe was close at his brother's heels.

The exit through which Vilnoff had disappeared refused to open. The wily fellow had locked it on the other side.

"Try the upstairs way!" suggested Joe.

The boys had now thrown caution to the winds. Frank wheeled around and ran up the basement stairs. He wrenched open the door at the top of the landing, and the two lads stepped through.

They found themselves in the kitchen of the house. Not a sound was to be heard from any part of the building. Vilnoff was nowhere to be seen.

As the Hardys stood there, undecided, the roar of a motor outside echoed suddenly. The boys ran to the back door. Through the glass panel they could see a car leaving the garage.

Frank and Joe were out of the house in a twinkling. By the time they had leaped from the porch the automobile was speeding down a lane toward the rear of the estate.

"Vilnoff must be in that car!" exclaimed Frank in disappointment.

"But how did he ever get to the garage?"

They went over to the small building to investigate. Their flashlights revealed a trap-door in the floor of the empty structure. Joe bent down and raised it, and as he did so the boys saw a flight of steps that lead to a passage below.

Frank descended the stairs to find an underground tunnel leading from the garage to the basement of Vilnoff's house. At the end of the passage he noticed a closed door; the key was still in the lock. The lad opened it and discovered, as he had suspected, that it led to the cellar of the house and was the very way by which the owner had fled when the Hardy boys had entered his workshop.

"I guess Vilnoff has escaped," said Joe, who had followed Frank into the basement. "There doesn't seem to be anyone else around the place, so we can have a good look at this shop of his."

On a nearby bench lay a sheaf of blue-prints. The boys examined them, and on the first set of plans they read:

"SUPER AERIAL BOMB." On another was inscribed, "MODEL B, SPECIAL MACHINE GUN." On a third, "SECRET—LIGHTWEIGHT TORPEDO FOR SUBMARINE USE."

The boys were astounded, and became even more so when a search of the basement revealed supplies of nitroglycerin, T. N. T., dynamite, gunpowder, guncotton, caps, fuses—enough deadly explosives to lay Bayport in ruins for blocks around. There was a model of a strange new type of machine gun under a tarpaulin in a corner. On the workbench was the shell of a bomb.

"So that's the secret of Vilnoff's place!" exclaimed Frank. "Inventions of warfare!"

"This is a matter for the police. No wonder the man ran away."

The boys went upstairs, and searched the

house high and low but the place was deserted. There was no trace of the butler, the gardener, or the chauffeur.

Joe went to the telephone and called Bayport police headquarters. He gave his name and then said:

"I think you had better send a couple of men down to stand guard over the Vilnoff residence tonight. Frank and I have made some mighty queer discoveries here."

"What's up?" asked the desk sergeant who had answered the phone.

"We've found a basement full of explosives. It looks as if Vilnoff has been using the house for inventing instruments of warfare."

"Whew!" exclaimed the officer in astonishment. "I'll send some men up there right away."

Joe put down the telephone.

"What's next?" he asked Frank.

"We must find Vilnoff and his cronies. I have a notion that the cabin in the clearing may be his hiding place."

"Shall we go there tonight?"

"Why not? That fellow may quit the country altogether, now that he knows the secret of his place has been discovered."

Joe agreed that this plan of procedure was entirely probable. Quick action was necessary. Although the Hardy boys could hardly realize

as yet the tremendous importance of the secret
upon which they had stumbled, they knew that
Vilnoff's possible presence at the cabin in the
clearing now took on a more sinister aspect.

"I think that place hides something a lot more
important than the temporary home of a stolen
horse," declared Frank. "Those tree signals
have been put in place for a definite purpose. I
think they were used when we were there to
warn the guards of our approach."

"Well," said Joe, "with what Dad told us,
and after seeing those cases unloaded from the
launch on the river, I suspect munitions."

"We'll have to prove that before we report
it," returned Frank.

"You're right," agreed his brother. "We
won't take any unnecessary risks, but we could
spy once again in the forbidden territory."

"Sure. Then bring in the police. We can't
let Vilnoff get away with his queer schemes any
longer."

The boys did not want to leave the man's
Bayport house until the police should arrive.
They were disappointed because Vilnoff had
tricked them and escaped through the secret
passageway, which doubtless had been prepared
for just such an emergency.

"Remember what Dad said at breakfast one
morning when we were talking about mysteries?" asked Joe. "He told us it was thought

that certain foreigners were buying munitions and concealing them in this country. I'll bet that's what Vilnoff has been mixed up in.''

''Probably he's the ringleader,'' Frank remarked.

Then a surprising thing happened. Every light in the house went out. Just as they did so the burglar alarm began ringing shrilly.

CHAPTER XVII

THE STRANGE MESSAGE

WHILE the bell was still ringing the Hardys heard heavy footsteps in the front hall. Then a gruff voice called out:

"Hi, there! What's going on?"

The boys switched on their flashlights and went to the front door. Two police officers were standing there. The alarm was still screeching madly.

The authorities had found the door unlocked and had entered without knocking. At the same moment the burglar alarm had been set into action. Frank reached out for the switch that controlled the signal and in a second the uproar ceased. Simultaneously the lights went on again.

"What's the matter? Who turned out the lights?" demanded one of the policemen. "What kind of a dump is this, anyway? The minute we opened the door they all went out and that bell began clangin' like mad."

"I guess some mechanism connected with the burglar alarm did it," said Frank.

"Well, what's all the trouble?" demanded the leader of the pair. "Let's have a look at this basement the sergeant was talking about."

Frank and Joe guided the men down to the cellar and showed them the plans and models they had discovered. They explained that they had been suspicious of Vilnoff, and had surprised him at work when, to all intents and purposes, he was supposed to be on his way to Europe. They related how he had escaped to the garage by the underground passage.

The policemen were impressed.

"You can just bet we'll guard this stuff. If anybody should get in here and touch any of it off it would blow half the town to pieces."

Frank and Joe said nothing of their own plans for going to the hide-out in the woods. Now that the house was under guard, with the policemen in readiness to apprehend Vilnoff and question him should he be unwary enough to return, they felt at liberty to leave and continue their own investigations.

When they left they held a council of war, discussing what their next move should be. Frank was all for setting out for the cabin in the woods at once, but another idea had occurred to Joe in the meantime.

"I think that mechanical tree gives them warning when anyone goes on the road near the place," he said. "Who knows but that

Vilnoff may have some guards here now, and we may be followed. I'd suggest that we try to throw them off the scent.''

"How?''

"You take the *Sleuth* up the river and wait for me in the inlet near the place where we were stalled when we saw the men unloading the boxes from the launch.''

"And what will you do?''

"I'll take the car and drive out to that gas station. I'll pretend something has gone wrong with the machine. I'll ask Gus for permission to use the telephone. I'll call you, supposedly, giving the impression that you are at home in Bayport.''

"I get it,'' said Frank. "It looks as if Gus and Pete have some connection with Vilnoff. You may learn a few things at the gas station in the bargain.''

"Perhaps. I'll merely use the telephone and say I've been delayed coming home. Then, after I leave I'll drive around to the inlet by one of the old roads back of the airport.''

The Hardy boys parted company outside the Vilnoff place and went their separate ways, Frank toward the boat-house where he tuned up the *Sleuth* for the night journey on the river, his brother toward their car, which he guided to the service station outside the city limits.

Joe's journey did not take very long, but on

the way he kept thinking about Gus. He was
fully convinced that the proprietor and Pete,
the truck-driver, knew more about Vilnoff and
his mysterious activities than either of them
would care to admit. In the back of the boy's
mind was the hope that his visit to the service
station might result in some clues of real value.

When the lights of the place appeared in
view Joe slowed down and brought his car to a
stop about a hundred feet from one of the gas
tanks. Then he got out, lifted the hood of the
roadster, and quickly disconnected a wire leading to the battery.

In a moment he walked toward the building
and was just about to open the door, when he
heard the ringing of a telephone inside. Soon
he heard the gruff voice of Gus calling:

"Hello!"

Then came a pause.

"Hello yourself," said the proprietor.

Another pause. Then the man remarked:

"Shake hands."

Joe heard a rattle as the receiver was put
back into place.

The lad could not make head nor tail of the
extraordinary conversation. "Shake hands!"
What did it mean?

It occurred to him that Gus might have been
speaking in accordance with a code previously
arranged between himself and the person who

had telephoned. This conviction only served to increase his suspicion that the proprietor and his gas station were not doing just the kind of business they appeared to be.

Joe waited a few moments, then banged noisily on the door. It was opened by Gus, who was in his shirt-sleeves. The man gave an exclamation of surprise when he recognized Joe.

"Hello," he said in a surly tone. "What do you want?"

"Something's wrong with my car," returned the lad. "I'd like to use your telephone, if you don't mind."

"I can't fix your car tonight," growled Gus.

"Well, then, I'll just have to leave it here, I suppose. I'm in a hurry. Let me use your phone and I'll get along."

The big fellow stepped back from the door.

"O. K.," he said. "You can use it if you like."

Joe stepped inside the place and went over to the telephone, calling the Hardy home. Gus stood leaning against the counter, evidently ready to hear anything that would be said. Soon Aunt Gertrude's snappy voice answered:

"Yes? Yes? Who is it?"

"Hello, is this Frank?" asked Joe.

"Frank?" snapped Aunt Gertrude. "Of course not. Don't you recognize a lady's voice when you hear it? Who is speaking?"

"Listen, Frank," continued Joe for the benefit of Gus but to the intense fury and bewilderment of Aunt Gertrude, "I'm at a service station just outside the city. The car is stalled and I'll have to leave it here all night."

"What on earth are you talking about?" clamored Aunt Gertrude. "Have you gone crazy? I'm not Frank and you know it. Frank isn't here——"

Joe ploughed on regardless.

"I'll be coming along presently, Frank. There ought to be a bus along in a few minutes. O. K.! So long, Frank!"

"If this is some kind of practical joke——" Aunt Gertrude was fuming, but Joe did not hear the rest of her sentence. He merely threw his worthy aunt into a positive rage by calmly hanging up the receiver.

"Thanks very much," he said to Gus. "Will you help me bring the car into your garage?"

The man nodded, and they went outside. Between them they pushed the roadster into the shelter. The proprietor did not volunteer to examine the car, nor did he appear to be at all appreciative of Joe's business.

"I'll be back for the machine tomorrow," Joe told him.

"All right," said Gus, and went into the station.

As Joe waited for the bus, he reflected that he

had learned nothing beyond the fact that Gus probably had made use of some sort of code in conversing by telephone with an unknown party. The other man might have been Vilnoff, or perhaps Pete, the truck-driver.

Eventually the lights of the bus appeared. The big vehicle came rolling swiftly down the highway and Joe walked across the road to get aboard. As he did so a truck rumbled up and stopped directly in front of the gas station. Joe recognized it at once.

It belonged to Pete!

The lad lost all interest in getting the bus. Already it had stopped, the door was open and the driver was waiting impatiently.

"Sorry," exclaimed Joe. "I've changed my mind."

The man at the wheel looked annoyed, then pulled away. The boy remained in the shadows and watched the truck. He saw someone climb down from the vehicle and hurry into the service station.

At that distance, and in the uncertain light, he could not be sure of the man's identity but he thought the fellow looked like Pete. As soon as the driver had disappeared into the building Joe scuttled across the road and crouched beneath a window. He was just in time to hear the voice of Gus.

"We've got something to worry about, I tell

you," the proprietor was saying. "I don't like the look of things."

"What's the matter?"

"I think you know what's the matter. Don't act so innocent with me. I'll bet you've gone and squealed."

"You're crazy!" snapped the other man. "Why should I squeal?"

"I think you did. I never did trust you, Pete——"

The sentence was left unfinished. Joe heard sounds of a scuffle. Then there came a cry, followed by a heavy crash.

A moment later the door was flung open violently and a man leaped across the threshold. Joe had barely time enough to slip back into the shadows out of sight. In the light that came streaming through the doorway he recognized Pete.

The driver flung himself out of the place, slamming the door behind him. He looked neither to right nor to left, but rushed over to his truck, jumped on board, and scrambled in behind the wheel. Inside of a few moments the vehicle was roaring down the highway.

Joe opened the door and peered inside the service station. Gus lay on the floor in front of the counter. He was unconscious, and there was a dark bruise on his forehead.

The Hardy boy went inside and knelt by the

man. He was alive, and evidently not seriously injured; simply knocked out for the time being.

Suddenly the phone rang sharply. Joe was undecided whether or not to answer it. Finally he concluded that he might take a chance, so got up and went over to the instrument. Imitating the voice of Gus as closely as he could, he growled:

"Hello!"

"Fifty-nine," answered a man's voice.

Joe recalled the strange conversation Gus had had previously. He risked the counter-sign.

"Hello yourself!"

"It may rain tomorrow," answered the other.

"Shake hands," said Joe.

Evidently his replies were considered quite satisfactory.

"All right. Road one is open."

"Road one?"

"*Yes. Death beyond the red hand. Be careful!*"

The other man rang off. Joe heard a groan. He looked around. Gus was stirring, regaining consciousness.

CHAPTER XVIII

THE STEALTHY SPEED-BOAT

Joe slipped quickly out of the room. Gus was not in need of help, and the boy had no desire for an interview with the man at that time.

How could he reach Frank, now that the bus was on its was to Bayport? The roadster provided the only answer to this problem.

He hurried into the garage. Fortunately Gus had not locked the door. Whipping out his flashlight, the lad hastily raised the hood of the car, replaced the detached wire, scrambled into the machine, and backed out. He then swung the auto around and sped away.

No one appeared at either the window or the door of the service station. Gus, still half stunned, evidently had heard nothing.

Joe thrust his foot down on the accelerator, making the car race down the highway. He wondered about his brother. What had happened to Frank Hardy?

Meanwhile that lad had steered the *Sleuth* down Barmet Bay, and then headed up Willow River, passing the airport. At a reduced rate of speed he had scanned the bank, searching for the inlet where they had seen the men unloading boxes from the speed-boat.

After consulting a map of the countryside near Bayport, and doing a little figuring on their own account, the Hardy boys had decided that the cabin in the clearing was somewhere in the locality of the inlet on Willow River. It was their conclusion that the place could be reached by roads from both the main highway and the river.

Frank's plan now was to wait for Joe, when both of them could look for a route to the mysterious clearing. The older lad anchored the *Sleuth* in the deep shadows of the inlet and sat down to wait.

"Might as well be doing something with my time," he said to himself. "I wonder if it would be of any use to explore that road where the men caught us?"

He left the boat and went ashore, using his flashlight sparingly to find his way. Vilnoff, or some member of his gang might be lurking about, and any light would certainly arouse curiosity.

Cautiously Frank advanced up the river bank. The night was dark and calm. He could hear no sound save the steady lapping of tiny waves on the beach. He blundered about in the weeds and thickets for some time before he finally emerged upon a road.

The lad looked back. There was still no sign of Joe.

"I'll go ahead a little distance anyway," Frank decided.

He trudged on up the dark road. At first it was little more than a trail, but later on it widened, and some deep ruts indicated that a truck had passed that way recently. He reflected that it probably was the one upon which the men had loaded the mysterious cases taken from the launch. Frank's intentions at first had been to proceed not more than a hundred yards or so, but as the road curved and wound through the woods before him he kept on.

Suddenly from a little distance ahead he heard a sound. He instantly dived toward a ditch and crouched among some dead leaves.

With wildly beating heart he waited, listening, scarcely daring to breathe. If any of Vilnoff's men should find him there the consequences would be unpleasant and perhaps fatal to his plans. The sound was not repeated, and Frank began to feel relieved.

His outstretched hand came in contact with a crumpled sheet of paper. He turned on the flashlight for a second, and in the brief moment of illumination he could see that it was marked with oddly scrawled lines broken by crosses in red ink.

Frank was interested. He picked up the

paper and got to his feet. Then he retired to the shelter of some bushes near by, where he could use the flashlight with little danger of its glow being seen by anyone who might chance to be coming down the road.

"This looks like a map!" he said to himself in growing excitement when he had examined the sheet again. The criss-cross lines were marked with various numbers, beginning at 1 and ending at 7. On one line he saw the scribbled words:

Danger—Electrically charged wire.

At the bottom of the plan was a raggedly indented line beneath which was written the one word, "river."

There was no doubt in Frank's mind that he had come upon a map that had been dropped by one of the men unloading cases from the speedboat. It indicated various roads, or paths, to a common destination. One of the lines ended at an inlet on the river—probably the very road he was now exploring.

With mounting excitement Frank continued his journey. About a quarter of a mile farther on he came to a fence, constructed of wire, and bearing a close resemblance to the one that had encircled the section of woods which the boys had entered at such great risk when they had found the hidden cabin.

Frank now remembered the warning on the

map he had just discovered—the warning that mentioned electrically charged wire. Perhaps it had reference to this very fence.

In the distance he thought he could see two figures moving about in the darkness. One of them was coming toward the fence. Frank crouched behind a clump of bushes.

The dark form came closer until at last a man was standing on the other side of the wire, only a few feet away from him. Then there was the flare of a match as the unknown lighted a cigarette.

A face was clearly revealed in the flicker. Frank gasped with surprise.

It was that of Ivan Evans, the jockey!

"Ivan!" Frank called out involuntarily.

The fellow started, looked around, then came closer to the netting.

"Who is it? Who's there?"

Ivan had spoken loudly, and Frank was in terror thinking he might have been heard by the other man in the enclosure, for he was sure he had seen someone other than the jockey.

"Quiet!" he whispered. "This is Frank Hardy."

"How did you get here?" asked Ivan in a low voice as the Hardy boy arose and approached the fence.

"How did *you* get here?" countered Frank.

"I was forced to come," replied the jockey.

"I couldn't help myself. Oh, if I could only get back to my riding. I don't know what they'll think of me at the race-track. I was due to report there and didn't show up, but it wasn't my fault."

"Joe and I thought something might have happened to you," said Frank. "We were afraid you had been kidnaped as we couldn't find any trace of you. Who brought you to this place?"

Ivan evaded the question.

"Will you help me get away?" he asked.

"Sure thing. Climb out and I'll have you in Bayport within half an hour."

"Good!"

Ivan reached out his hands toward the wire.

"Careful!" Frank said suddenly. "Those wires may be charged with electricity."

"Not this part," Ivan replied. "I've been told about those charged ones. It's safe here. I'll shin over——"

Just then they heard a gruff voice call out, "Ivan!" and heavy footsteps sounded nearby. Someone was running toward them.

Frank dodged into hiding again. The jockey began climbing the enclosure, but in his haste part of his clothing caught on the barbs. Then a bright, powerful flashlight was turned on him and he stood plainly revealed in its merciless glare.

"Hey, there!" shouted a gruff voice. "Come down off that wire. I see you. Tryin' to make a getaway, huh?"

There was no hope. Ivan was caught in the very act of trying to escape. A burly figure rushed up and grabbed him by the collar, pulling him off the fence.

"None o' that!" growled his captor. "You want the boss to kill me? He told me not to let you out of his cabin. I thought I could trust you. The minute I let you out for a little walk and a breath o' fresh air you try to make a getaway. Huh!"

The man hustled the young fellow away. Frank heard him say:

"Just for that you'll be locked up now. I can't take any chances on your running away. Come along!"

Frank was disappointed. Had the jockey only managed to escape, the Hardy boy was sure he would have had plenty of information to give. Maybe Vilnoff was his kidnaper! However, something had been gained. He knew now that Ivan was imprisoned behind the netting, perhaps in the clearing shack, and Frank felt that the rescue of the boy could be accomplished easily enough, once help was obtained.

Frank decided to go back to the inlet and see if Joe had shown up. Perhaps he and his

brother together might be able to raid the forbidden fenced-in area and rescue Ivan.

The Hardy boy lost no time in retracing his
footsteps down the dark road, hastening toward
the river in the hope that Joe might be there
waiting for him. He just reached the end of
the trail and was hurrying down the bank, when
he heard a faint, muffled throbbing out on the
water. Swiftly a dark shape shot around the
end of the point, and came racing toward the
shore.

It was a speed-boat, its motors so muffled that
it was traveling almost in silence. Frank flung
himself back of some bushes just as the oncoming craft slowed down and nosed its way quietly
inshore. He could hear voices and see the vague
shadows of two men.

One of them climbed out of the boat. The
other remained in the launch. There was the
subdued sound of bumping and banging, and
a heavy case was handed over the side. The
man on shore received it, hoisted it onto his
shoulders, and began trudging up toward the
road.

Frank was glad he had hidden himself, for
the stranger passed him not three feet away.
A few minutes later the other man came up
from the boat, in like manner burdened by a
heavy case which he carried on up the trail,
following his companion.

"If those kegs hold munitions," said Frank to himself, "I'll just get some evidence!"

He got up and hurried down to the speed-boat. Climbing on board, he found about a dozen cases covered with a big piece of canvas. He flung the cloth aside and tried to lift one of the boxes. It was very heavy. He had difficulty in moving it, but eventually worked it up onto the side of the craft. He gave it a push, and the weighty object toppled over into the water with a loud splash.

Then Frank became greatly dismayed, for up on the river bank he could hear voices.

"Thought I heard a splash!" a man said. "Let's have a look!"

CHAPTER XIX

ROAD NUMBER ONE

THE men were coming back!

Obviously they had not carried their two cases all the way up the road, as Frank had figured on, but had most likely left them in hiding, to be picked up by a truck later on.

The boy was trapped!

He tried to get out of the boat in the hope of stepping on shore before the men should find him, but in his haste he tripped over the end of one of the cases and fell sprawling. By the time he had picked himself up he could hear the footsteps of those at the top of the slope.

Fortunately the night was very dark. Frank had only one chance now. He leaped to the back of the craft, balanced himself for a moment, then dropped into the water. Although he made every effort to escape noiselessly, there was a slight splash as he slid over the side.

"There!" one of the men said. "I heard it again. There's something wrong in the boat."

"I heard it, too," answered the other.

As they hurried to the speed-boat, Frank could hear them stumbling over the rocks. He waited no longer, but submerged himself and began to swim under water.

It was bitterly cold, and the boy was hampered by his clothing. He could hear the men clumping into the boat. If he should come to the surface now they would surely see him.

Frank swam steadily under water. He held his breath until he thought his lungs would burst. At last he could stand it no longer and popped to the surface, inhaling deeply of fresh air.

He was now a good distance from the launch. Through the gloom he could dimly see the two men standing in the craft and looking over the side. Fortunately they were not gazing in Frank's direction.

"That's queer," one of them was saying. "I was sure I heard two splashes."

"And what's more," said the other, "I felt certain that we had twelve cases left in the boat, and now there are only eleven."

"You must have counted 'em wrong. Let's get busy and unload 'em."

Apparently the men were satisfied that there was nothing amiss, for they resumed their task of moving the boxes and carrying them up to the road.

Frank swam on toward the *Sleuth*. He was chilled to the bone and exhausted from the weight of his sodden clothing when at last he reached the craft and pulled himself over the side.

He lay in the bottom of the boat until he had regained his strength. Then he remembered that in one of the lockers were a pair of old trousers, a ragged sweater, and some rubber sneakers. He had tossed all these into the compartment after a fishing trip during the summer, not thinking that they would be of use in such an emergency.

Frank opened the locker and found the garments. Although disreputable in appearance, they were dry, so he quickly peeled off his wet clothes and changed into the others. Then, his teeth chattering, he sat in the *Sleuth* to await the arrival of Joe.

At the far end of the inlet he could hear the two men unloading the speed-boat. The operation took some time, but finally it was finished. Then the strangers got back into their boat and pushed off from shore. The muffled drumming of their motor again sounded in the night, and Frank saw the dark shape of the sinister craft glide out toward the open river.

At the same time he caught the gleam of a flashlight among the bushes. His own was soaked through, so he could not have answered the signal had he wanted to. It occurred to him, however, that the flare might have been made by someone from the clearing at the end of the road, so he remained quiet. Presently he heard footsteps approaching along the shore, and Joe's voice called out softly:

"Are you there, Frank?"

"Right! I've been waiting for you," exclaimed his brother in relief. "What in the world happened? I was just about to give up and go looking for you."

"And where did you get those clothes?"

Joe told Frank about his experiences at the service station. His brother, in turn, related the momentous news of how he had found Ivan, seen the men in the speed-boat, and made the discovery of the map.

"Let's have a look at it! Maybe we'll have something to work on now," said Joe.

By the gleam of the flashlight they examined the paper. Then Joe recalled the strange message he had heard over the telephone.

"Road one is open. Death beyond the red hand. Be careful."

He noted the spot marked I on the map.

"I don't know what the fellow meant by the red hand, but we're safe enough following Road Number One, I imagine. Why, according to this map that leads right out of this inlet. Let's go!"

They scrambled from the boat and made their way up the shore, then on the trail toward the fence where Frank had encountered Ivan, the jockey. When they reached it Joe was all for climbing over at once but his brother was cautious.

"It wasn't electrically charged when Ivan tried to scale it, but they may have turned on the current since," he said. "I think we had better test it."

Frank took a metal key from his pocket and dropped it on top of one of the wire strands. There was a snapping blue flash the moment it came in contact with the wire.

"Just as I thought," he remarked, picking up the key from the ground. "It's lucky you didn't try it, Joe."

The road ran along the side of the netting, so they followed it, hoping to find a gate through which they might gain entrance to the enclosure. They came across none, although they searched for five minutes. However, they discovered a place where the wires appeared to be overrun with weeds, creepers, and small bushes. Joe examined the ground at this point by the gleam of the flashlight.

"I see something that looks mighty like the track of a truck," he said. "But it seems to lead directly toward the fence."

"I have a hunch," remarked Frank. "Those

creepers don't look natural here, when the rest of the enclosure is bare.''

He stripped away some of the vegetation. As he had thought, he found a camouflaged gate. Before trying to open it, however, he tested it with his key. This time there was no flash of electricity, so the boys knew that the gate, at least, was not charged. They did not bother to open it, but simply climbed over and dropped into a field beyond.

Some distance away they spied a dark hulk against the background of the clearing, and went over toward it.

"A cabin," said Joe.

The place was in darkness. The Hardy boys crept stealthily forward. Perhaps this was the shack in which Ivan was imprisoned. Yet they could hear no sound from the building. On further investigation they discovered a door hanging wide open so they walked boldly in and found the building to be empty.

"There may be half a dozen cabins around here, for all we know," remarked Joe. "We still haven't found the one where you saw the Negro driver and Vilnoff's shadow through the window."

Suddenly Frank caught sight of a twinkling gleam among the trees.

"Perhaps we're on the right track now," he said quietly. "Let's follow that light."

The clearing gave way to woods now and the boys plunged into it, heading toward that tantalizing gleam. Joe sniffed the air.

"I smell hay!" he exclaimed.

"What of it?"

"Hay means horses. Maybe——"

They emerged from the woods into another small clearing, and found a tiny cabin. The light they had seen came from a lantern hanging just inside the open doorway. The boys stole cautiously over and peered inside.

The place was an improvised stable. Lying on the floor was a horse—a sleek, splendid animal that suddenly opened his eyes, saw the boys, and scrambled to his feet. Frank gave a cry of delight.

"*Topnotch!*" he whispered excitedly.

It was indeed the missing race-horse. Frank easily recognized the animal from the pictures he had seen of it in the newspapers and from the description given by Mr. Prescott.

Topnotch seemed to feel that he was with friends. He gave a whinny, and nuzzled against the boys as they hurried into the stable.

"Well, this clears up one of our mysteries at any rate," declared Frank, stroking the animal's silky mane. "We've found *Topnotch!*"

"But how to get him out of here—that's the problem," declared Joe.

Suddenly there was a terrific crash!

The Hardy boys turned around, alarmed. Then they saw that the door of the stable had swung shut. Joe sprang toward it, lunging his body against its weight. It did not budge.

A heavy bar on the outside was in place, effectually locking them in!

CHAPTER XX

"I wonder if that happened by accident or on purpose," said Frank in a low voice.

"Accident, I think," returned Joe. "There was a bar on the outside. Probably it fell into place when the door blew shut."

Regardless of the cause, the Hardy boys were thoroughly locked in. They had found the missing race-horse, only to be made prisoners themselves. Pleased as they were to have found *Topnotch,* their predicament seemed serious, for if any of the kipnapers were to come along the lads would be in a bad way.

"We've got to get out of here," said Joe. "There's not one window. Let's look around."

They searched the cabin thoroughly, but as it was built of stout logs there seemed to be no way of escape. The roof was firm, and there was no chimney. Finally the boys tested the floor.

Here they had luck. One of the boards was loose, and when they pried it up they were able to get hold of the next one and work it

166

free as well. When a space had been cleared, Joe crawled into the opening and switched on his flashlight.

"It's O.K., Frank," he announced. "There's a hole at the back of the shack."

Joe began crawling beneath the building and Frank quickly followed suit. In a short time they emerged from under the structure and found themselves free once more.

They examined the door that had slammed shut. Joe was of the opinion that the whole thing had been an accident and that the wind had merely blown it closed, but Frank was dubious. He wondered if someone had seen them entering the place and then deliberately dropped the cross-bar to imprison them.

"We're out now, and that's all that matters," said Joe philosophically. "We must locate Ivan, though."

"Boy!" exclaimed Frank. "I'm mighty glad we've found *Topnotch!*"

"We're not home yet," Joe reminded him. "If we happen to get caught, they'll just move the horse somewhere else and we'll be no farther ahead than we were."

"We won't get caught," returned Frank confidently.

They went across the clearing and entered the woods again. They now searched at random, without the faintest idea of the direction in which they were headed. It was hard going, traveling through the dense thickets, with undergrowth and bushes tripping the boys up as they floundered in the darkness.

Their flashlight was of little use to them, for the vegetation was a dark, solid mass. Besides, they did not want to show a light more often than was absolutely necessary.

The trees began to thin out at last, giving way to another clearing. In the open space straight ahead was a cabin.

"I wonder if Ivan is there?" whispered Joe.

"Can't see any light."

"Don't take any chances. The place may not be as deserted as it looks."

They drew nearer, and saw that there was no window on that side of the shack. The boys circled warily around until they reached another corner of the building. A dim light shone from a small window.

The Hardys were convinced now that they had discovered Ivan's place of imprisonment. Cautiously they stole forward.

To their disappointment they found that the window had been covered with a piece of sacking on the inside. It was impossible to see through it. However, they could hear someone talking.

"You might as well go to sleep, kid," said a man in gruff tones.

Another voice answered, but it was so muffled that Frank and Joe could not distinguish any words.

"There's no chance of escape for you, Ivan Evans," came the reply a moment later. "If you go outside you'll be caught. We don't figger on lettin' you leave until we're good and ready."

Again the muffled voice. The boys strained their ears, but still were unable to make out the words.

"It won't get you nowhere sittin' beside the fireplace all night. Go to sleep," growled the jockey's captor.

The Hardy boys heard nothing more for a time but later they could distinguish a deep, rumbling snore. Apparently the older man had followed his own advice and had gone to sleep.

"How are we going to get word to Ivan?" whispered Joe. "We don't want to take a chance on awakening that other fellow."

Frank had a plan.

"There's no smoke coming from the chimney," he said. "From what the fellow said, I think Ivan must be sitting in front of the fireplace. We may be able to get a message to him that way."

He took a sheet from Joe's notebook and scribbled a hasty message. It read:

"We're outside, Ivan, and will come back

later to rescue you. Be ready. If you want us
to do this, make a scraping sound in the fireplace. H.B.''

He showed the note to Joe.

''Those are not your initials,'' said his
brother. ''What's the idea of signing it
'H.B.'?''

''Hardy Boys, of course,'' answered Frank.

He wrapped the paper around a small stone,
tied it securely in place with a bit of string,
then stood back and looked at the cabin. The
ends of the logs appeared to offer the best means
of reaching the roof. Joe stood guard to give
warning in case anyone should approach, or
if Ivan's guard should hear a noise and come
out to investigate.

Frank began his climb, and made it without
any trouble. Silently he crawled toward the
chimney. Then he dropped the note and stone
down the opening. He heard it fall with a
sharp clatter into the fireplace beneath.

Frank held his breath in suspense. Had the
noise disturbed the guard? There came no
sound from within the cabin for a long time.
Then, from the fireplace he heard a slow, grat-
ing noise. It stopped, but was repeated again.
Frank was assured that Ivan had received his
message and that he wanted to be rescued.

He crawled back to the end of the roof and
lowered himself quietly to the ground.

"It worked, Joe! Ivan will be ready when we come back."

"Why not try to get him out now?"

"We've a lot of detective work to do yet. Remember we started out to find Vilnoff. I want to learn what he's up to and what's in those cases. If we rescue Ivan now we may be followed and forced to make a quick getaway."

Frank stole silently across the clearing, with Joe close at his heels.

CHAPTER XXI

THE SINISTER SIGN POST

THE Hardy boys had made great progress, but the mystery was still far from being cleared up. They had located the missing race-horse, discovered Ivan, paved the way for the jockey's rescue, and had found the secret of Vilnoff's basement workshop. Nevertheless, much remained to be done.

Neither the ringleader nor any of his helpers had been arrested. The mystery of the sinister speed-boat and the heavy cases remained unsolved. The real reason behind the elaborate system of signals, charged wires, and hidden roads of the forbidden territory had not yet been uncovered.

Now that they were actually inside the lines, Frank felt that they had a good chance of learning a great deal more than they already knew. But what should they do now? Which way should they turn to find clues which would aid the authorities?

"I wonder if we could find that road we took when we escaped in the truck," suggested Joe.

"That goes past the cabin where Vilnoff was."

"Let's have another look at that map I found," suggested Frank.

When they were well out of sight of the cabin he took the sheet from his pocket, and the two examined it by the rays of the flashlight.

"There's Road Number One, where we came up from the inlet," Frank pointed out. "That red cross must be the clearing where *Topnotch* is hidden. This cross must indicate the place we just left. And here are some more little crosses over to the right."

"Let's push on in that direction, then," Joe decided.

They plunged through the thickets. Twigs and dry brush snapped and crackled noisily underfoot. Presently they came to a winding path which made progress easier.

"I can't understand," said Frank, "why Ivan is being kept here. What's behind it all?"

"Perhaps the kidnapers were encouraged when they got the ransom money for *Topnotch* and thought Mr. Prescott would pay for the return of his jockey, too."

"Maybe. But he's not likely to pay a second ransom—not after having been swindled out of his money the first time."

"It will be too bad if we're caught before we have a chance to rescue Ivan and the horse," Joe remarked. "We've done pretty well up to now, but all our work will have been for nothing if we should get tripped up. They would just move the horse and the jockey somewhere else and we'd have to start all over again.''

''Maybe we wouldn't have a chance to do that. This is a mysterious gang we are following. What was that message you heard over the telephone? 'Death beyond the red hand!' ''

''You're right,'' agreed Joe. ''I wonder what that message meant, after all. Do you think we'll run into any real trouble?''

''I'm sure we must be careful. If Vilnoff is engaged in a munitions plot he and his helpers will certainly try to keep intruders away.''

They continued along the winding path. Suddenly Joe stopped short.

''Listen!'' he whispered.

The boys stood motionless.

''What's the matter?'' asked Frank.

''I thought I heard a noise on the path behind us. It sounded like someone running.''

They waited, but could hear nothing. Joe finally concluded that his imagination must have been playing tricks on him.

''I guess I was just hearing things,'' he said sheepishly.

''Not getting nervous, are you?'' laughed his brother.

A few minutes later Joe stopped again. This

time he flung himself beside the trail and put
his ear to the ground.

"I was right, Frank!" he said tensely when
he got up. "There *is* someone following us."

"More than one person?"

"Yes. I could hear them plainly."

"Let's hurry."

A minute later Frank stumbled and almost
fell headlong. As his hands struck the ground
they encountered a heavy metal ring. When he
regained his balance, he and Joe examined the
ring and found that it was the handle to a trap-
door.

"Maybe we could hide here until they pass,"
Joe suggested.

Frank gave the door a yank, and leaped back
in dismay. A menacing face had appeared and
a stream of angry words in a foreign tongue
greeted the startled boys. The face disappeared
and Joe instinctively yelled:

"After him."

"No," Frank warned. "There may be a
gang of them there and we'd be putting ourselves at their mercy. We'd better go on."

Joe saw the wisdom of his brother's suggestion and regretfully suppressed his desire to see
where the trap-door might lead.

"Come on!"

They hustled down the path as quickly as they
dared. Far behind them they could detect the

sharp snapping of branches and a heavy thudding of footsteps. Somehow their presence in the forbidden territory must have been discovered.

Soon they noticed the sound of running water immediately ahead. The trail dipped sharply. Frank switched on his flashlight. A wide brook barred their way.

"How about wading it?" Joe said.

"It's too cold and deep. We'd be drenched to the skin if we were to try it. There must be a bridge or a fallen tree along this creek somewhere."

There was nothing to do but follow the stream.

"Which way?" asked Joe.

"If we go downstream we'll probably reach the river soon."

"Downstream it is, then."

It was more difficult to walk because there was no path along the bank. Dry leaves and twigs crackled loudly under foot. Frank had to keep the flashlight turned on almost constantly to light their way. The batteries had not been renewed in some time, and gradually the rays grew dimmer until finally they went out altogether.

"That *would* happen!" muttered the boy in disgust.

"It's a good thing I thought of putting

an extra battery into my pocket,'' said Joe.

He took the flashlight from his brother and was just fixing it, when his foot caught on a root. He lurched, and grabbed at a small tree to save himself from falling into the creek. As he did so, the battery flew out of his hand. He made a frantic lunge, but it bounded from a rock and splashed into the swift water.

The Hardy boys were left in pitch darkness. The loss of their means of illumination was a disastrous blow. Joe bitterly condemned himself for his clumsiness.

"It wasn't your fault," Frank assured him. "I should have been quick enough to have grabbed it."

They went on. Frank lit matches so that they could get their bearings from time to time, but they made only slow progress. Behind them they could hear the steady snapping of twigs and threshing of branches as their pursuers drew closer on their heels.

At last, however, the boys emerged from the dense vegetation onto an open road. They had been plunging along parallel to it all the while.

"Ah, this is better!" declared Frank. "I wonder where the route leads to?"

"It doesn't matter as long as it brings us somewhere. Listen—I can hear the men again. They aren't very far behind."

They could detect the heavy footsteps **very** plainly as they came down the road.

Frank struck another match. The stream lay immediately ahead, and was spanned at this point by a small wooden bridge. As the Hardy boys hurried toward it a shout came from behind them.

"No use!" Frank gasped. "We'll **never** make it. They'll catch up to us in no time. We had better hide."

He grabbed Joe by the arm and sprang for a deep hollow among the thickets beside the road. They were not a moment too soon. Hardly had they concealed themselves among the dead leaves and bushes than the whole scene was revealed by a brilliant light.

The searchers, carrying a powerful flash, had just come around the bend in the road. The glare of the beam revealed the bridge, the stream, and the trees beyond. It also showed them something else—something that gave the boys a thrill of astonishment.

Upon the bridge was an enormous sign post, which differed from any they had ever seen. It was in the shape of a huge hand that looked human. Had it not been for its size, it might have given the illusion of a real one mounted on top of the post.

From their hiding place the Hardy boys gazed

at the sinister sign post in amazement. Why had it been placed there? What did it mean?

"They didn't cross the bridge," said a voice behind them suddenly. "They must be hidden here somewhere. Scatter around and search the bushes."

Evidently there were several men in the pursuing party. Frank and Joe could hear them crashing about among the thickets.

"Maybe we had better run for it," Joe whispered.

"They'd be sure to see us and put an end to our sleuthing."

The gleams of no less than three flashlights could be discerned through the darkness.

Suddenly Frank saw to his horror that the strange sign post was moving! It turned! Then the fingers began twitching!

"Gosh! Do you see that?" whispered Joe.

The hand swung around and stopped. The index finger shot out. Then it turned downward until it pointed directly toward the hiding place of the boys.

For a moment they were almost paralyzed by fear. They could not understand the mechanism of the monstrous sign post, but they had seen enough to know that it would reveal their presence to the searchers.

The men were drawing closer and closer as

they beat their way through the brush. Frank started to crawl out of the hollow, and Joe followed close behind him.

"When I give the word, get ready to run!" Frank whispered.

The two crouched at the edge of the ditch.

"O.K.," snapped Frank.

The Hardy boys sprang to their feet and leaped up onto the road. They raced swiftly toward the bridge. Luck was with them at first. They knew they were not being seen, for they could hear no outcry from behind them.

The boys reached the bridge. Then something strange and terrifying happened.

The hand of the sinister sign post turned red! With the dreadful finger pointing straight at the boys, the hand changed swiftly from white to a deep crimson.

"Frank! Stop!" cried Joe. "Remember the message I heard over the telephone!"

Death beyond the red hand!

CHAPTER XXII

THE MAD INVENTOR

DEATH in front of them—certain capture behind them!

The Hardy boys faced one of the worst dilemmas in their careers as amateur detectives. They halted indecisively beneath the sign post that glowed red above them.

"We don't dare go ahead!" gasped Joe. "The hand is a warning."

"If we go back, those men will catch us, and we'll lose everything we've already accomplished!"

The boys could see the gleaming flashlights in the thickets, swinging back and forth as their pursuers prowled about in search of them. Suddenly there came a yell from one of the men.

"Hey, look! The hand has turned red!" he cried.

"Someone on the bridge!" shouted another. "Yes—I can see them. There they are. After 'em, boys!"

One of the flashlights swung around and cast a long, narrow beam of white light which fell

181

directly on the Hardys. There was a roar of exultation from the men.

"We'll have to take a chance," decided Frank. "The sign post warning may be only a bluff."

"We'll soon find out," panted Joe, as he and his brother came to a decision. "The men won't follow if they know there's death on the other side. Let's see what they do, before we give up to them."

Instantly the boys rushed under the red hand, their feet thudding on the planks of the bridge. As they reached the far side they hid near the water and got out of range of the brilliant searchlights. They waited breathlessly for their pursuers to follow.

But the men did not follow; in fact, they suddenly seemed to abandon the search. For the first time in a long while, the Hardy boys became panic-stricken.

"I guess we've come too far."

"Grab my hand," urged Frank. "We don't want to become separated in the darkness. And we're not going a step farther. We're going back!"

The two boys arose and started toward the bridge. Just then a dull light illuminated the area dimly. Through the haze Frank and Joe could discern a figure stalking toward them down a road.

"Let's run," gasped the younger Hardy.

Their first step was interrupted by a piercing howl and the most blood-curdling laughter they had ever heard. Then a high-pitched voice called out:

"Stand where you are!"

Frank and Joe gasped, for they recognized the oncoming man. He was Vilnoff! But not Vilnoff as they had known him, suave, gentlemanly. Now he was wild-eyed, with the malign look of a trapped animal.

"Stand where you are!" he repeated, and now halted in front of the boys. "I am master here!" he shouted, waving his arms. "My word is law!"

Frank and Joe had recovered from their fright and now faced the man boldly.

"You can't bluff us," said Joe. "We've found you out!"

"You're through, Vilnoff," added Frank quietly. "The game is up. We know where *Topnotch*, the race-horse, is hidden. We know where Ivan is being kept prisoner."

Vilnoff laughed sardonically.

"Ach, Ivan, yes," he said. "A fine boy. An egcellent lad."

"Why did you kidnap him?" demanded Joe.

"For his own good," retorted Vilnoff. "But you—you ask questions. Dot vill gain you nodding. I haf you vhere I vant you now."

He burst into another peal of hideous and maniacal laughter. The boys knew now that Vilnoff was a madman—a dangerous lunatic.

"I tried to be nice to you," he said. "I did not vant you to be my enemies. But you have pursued me relentlessly."

"And why not?" said Frank sternly. "You have been inventing machines of warfare, probably to be used against our country."

Vilnoff glanced at them cunningly.

"I am not a bad man as you think," he said. "But I hate Bayport!"

He snapped out the words viciously.

"I hate your whole country!" he repeated with sinister emphasis.

"Why do you live here, then?" asked Joe.

"I stay here only for the purpose of revenge," declared Vilnoff. "My vife—the best and finest woman who ever lived—she vas an American. But an American killed her! Right in Bayport! She gave her life for a man who is in Washington now trying to urge your government to harm my country."

His voice rose to a shout.

"So I hate your land, and I have intended to make war on it!" he yelled, his eyes blazing as he shook both fists at the boys.

"Single-handed?" demanded Frank in outright astonishment.

The Hardy boys had felt, from hints their

father had given, that perhaps Vilnoff was a
secret agent for some foreign power. To learn
that the mad inventor had conceived his diabolical schemes alone and for no reason save
personal spite was something they had never
considered.

"Ach! Single-handed! It vas clever, vas
it not?" asked Vilnoff boastfully. "All my fine
system of lights and wires and signals. You
have seen some of dem. I had a great scheme.
I vas going to make hidden places like dis one
in all parts of your country."

Frank, sparring for time until he might de-
cide the best way to handle this insane man,
concluded to ask a direct question.

"You have a lot of munitions stored here.
Aren't you afraid they'll blow up before you
are ready?"

Vilnoff sneered.

"Dey are vell hidden. Dey obey *my* com-
mands vhen to explode."

Then he shook his head regretfully.

"But you have ruined my big plan. My
scheme—it can never be finished. You have
broken it up."

"And we're mighty glad of it!" declared
Frank. "Why don't you come along with us
now? We'll see that nothing dreadful happens
to you," he added, knowing that the place for
this strange individual was an asylum.

Vilnoff glared at the boys.

"I cannot do vhat I vant to," said the maniac softly, "but I can do a great deal. I can blow up this whole territory. I can cause great suffering in your beloved Bayport and that hateful Spurtown that have caused me such suffering. And what's more," he snarled, *"I am going to do it!"*

The man turned swiftly and sped away before the boys could stop him. Quickly they dashed after him, but in a few moments the strange light vanished and they were left in total darkness.

"What'll we do?" gasped Joe. "Do you think Vilnoff meant what he said?"

"He's mad enough to try," replied Frank. *"We must stop him!"*

"But how? We don't know which way to go."

The older Hardy came to a quick decision. "This is too big a job for us, Joe, to tackle alone. We must get help."

"We'll be captured by Vilnoff's men if we go back."

"We'll tell them the truth," suggested Frank. "They won't want to be blown to bits. It's our best bet."

As the boys spun around to retrace their steps they noticed a tiny red gleam just off the road they were on. Frank stepped into the

thicket to take a look. Joe heard him murmur
"Oh," and followed his brother. He, too,
gurgled an involuntary "Uh."

The two Hardys had stepped into some kind
of a very deep opening in the earth, and were
falling down into an unknown abyss.

CHAPTER XXIII

THE SECRET DOOR

FRANK and Joe were stunned by their impact with the solid ground. Fortunately for them it was nothing but earth, so no bones were broken. Moreover, the younger boy had not landed on top of his brother, so any injury on that account had been avoided.

Joe was the first to regain his wits. "Frank, are you all right?" he asked in a tense voice.

There was no answer for a few moments. Then Frank murmured, "Joe? Oh, I'm glad you're here. But where are we? Gosh, my head hurts."

"Badly?" questioned Joe with a sinking feeling.

"No. Be O. K. in a few minutes. But where are we?"

"At the bottom of a hole in Vilnoff's enclosure," replied Joe.

"Oh, yes!" said Frank, suddenly in full possession of his faculties. "I remember now. He said he is going to blow up the place. We must get out of here and report him!"

"Wish I had a light," complained Joe.

"Come to think of it, I guess I have some matches."

"Don't strike any!" begged Frank. "You recall Vilnoff admitted munitions are hidden here. Right now we may be next to some."

His surmise was well taken. As the boys began to feel around in their dark prison, their fingers came into contact with boxes piled up. Suddenly Frank's hand, feeling along a stone wall, touched a switch. Immediately the place was lighted up.

"An arsenal!" cried Joe, looking around.

The boys found themselves standing at the entrance to a wide subterranean room. On either side of a narrow aisle cases of bullets were piled to the ceiling, which was about six feet high. They were plainly labelled "Machine Gun Bullets," "Rifle Bullets," "Revolver Bullets," with various numbers to indicate their size.

"Let's get out of here," urged Joe.

But how were they to do it? The entrance by which the boys had come in so unexpectedly was no longer open. To their horror they found that an iron door covered the hole. It had been securely fastened from the outside, making escape impossible.

"Trapped!" yelled Joe.

"Maybe there's an exit at the other end," exclaimed Frank, racing along the narrow passage between the boxes. "Here's a door," he cried in exultation.

On the side wall he found a lever, which he pushed. The iron door slid open noiselessly, revealing a long, narrow passage. To the disappointment of the Hardys they saw no opening to the outside.

"Wonder what's ahead of us?" queried Joe as he hurried along after his brother.

Frank was already moving a lever, which controlled the exit.

"More ammunition," he called over his shoulder, as he stepped into a storeroom beyond.

The place was filled with wooden cases of rifles, but the boys did not stop to examine them. Their minds had but a single thought: to escape and if possible stop the mad inventor from carrying out his plans. After racing through another storage place filled with bombs, both lads held unvoiced ideas too fearful for words.

But a surprise awaited them at the end of a third narrow tunnel. As the door which led from it opened, a bell began to ring.

"Shut it quick!" cried Joe.

Frank did so, but his action made no difference. In a moment the door opened again. Framed in the opening, and looking at them with a sardonic smile, was Vilnoff! He gave vent to a cackling, demented laugh when he saw the boys.

"So!" he gloated. "You still try to stop me! But it is too late!"

With that the door closed quickly. Hurriedly Frank pushed the wall lever on his side, but this time it did not seem to work. Joe groaned. In a moment, however, the mechanism slowly responded.

"He's gone!" cried Frank.

The boys found themselves in a large room filled with machinery which was set firmly in a concrete floor. A brilliant electric light illuminated every corner of the place.

Vilnoff was nowhere in sight. The Hardys saw a closed steel door at the other side of the room, but at first their attempts to open it were futile.

"He must have gone through there, I'm sure," Frank declared thoughtfully.

A row of push-buttons beside the door attracted Joe's attention.

"Perhaps one of these controls the opening and closing," he suggested.

Joe pushed the first button. Instantly all the lights in the chamber went out, leaving the boys in total darkness. Hastily the lad switched them on again.

He tried the next one. A giant motor at the far end of the room began to hum, throwing off blue sparks. Joe turned it off and pushed the button below.

Slowly the big steel door began to move. **On** well-oiled hinges it slid open silently before them, revealing another room beyond.

The boys hurried through the doorway. They were scarcely over the threshold when the big hinge began swinging back, thudding shut softly behind them.

"Caught!" cried Frank in alarm.

"Automatic electric control, I guess," said Joe. "There must be another device for re-opening the door."

Vilnoff was not in the second room. The place was filled with switches, a great maze of electric wiring, several dynamos, transformers and similar equipment. A safety rail ran around the formidable array.

Like the previous place, this one, too, was equipped with a steel door controlled by an electric button. The boys debated whether they should go ahead.

"No use turning back," declared Frank. "If Vilnoff went through that door we'll follow him and track him down if we can. It's too late to get help from the outside."

"O.K.," said Joe. "I'm with you."

He found the proper switch, and the door swung open before them. The moment they were in the next chamber it closed automatically.

This compartment was smaller, and contained

only a switchboard and a telephone. A hasty examination revealed the fact that all the signs, alarms and charged wires guarding the forbidden territory could be controlled from this one centre.

"What a layout!" exclaimed Frank, taking stock of the situation. "This place is a regular fortress."

"But where's Vilnoff?"

"There is still another door."

Frank then examined the switchboard more closely. One of the signs was marked "Red Hand Sign Post." Another read, "Storage Vault No. 1." A third controlled "Electric Wiring—East Side," and so on, covering all parts of the fence surrounding the property. One of them was labeled "Artificial Tree."

Joe tried the push-button beside the opening to the control room. It clicked. The door swung open, revealing a room beyond. But it was in total darkness!

"He probably switched off the light as he went through," Frank suggested. "We'll go on in."

"Be careful!" warned Joe. "Vilnoff is no doubt armed."

Frank stepped boldly across the threshold with Joe behind him. Then, echoing through the chamber, they heard a hideous, high-pitched laugh, that ended in a scream of exultation.

Abruptly the whole chamber was flooded with light. There, before them, stood Vilnoff!

He was standing with his back to the far wall, facing the boys. Directly before him was a row of formidable iron levers, on two of which his hands rested. The Hardys started forward and would have seized the man, but he snarled so menacingly that they halted.

"Back!" rasped the eccentric foreigner. "Stand back, you fools! Each von of dese levers is connected with switches. I am vaiting now—for de first explosion dat vill blow up dis place and make great trouble in your beloved Bayport!"

As the horrified boys watched, Vilnoff glanced at an electric clock on the wall.

"In twenty minutes," he said triumphantly, "dere vill be an explosion. At each succeeding ten minutes dere vill follow anodder."

Frank made an involuntary lunge toward the levers.

"Don't touch dem!" yelled Vilnoff. "It is too late now. Dey are set. I am smart, but I must die. You are smart boys, but you must die with me!"

CHAPTER XXIV

THE RIDE AGAINST DEATH

The Hardy boys realized that there was nothing to be lost and perhaps everything to be gained if they would make a desperate effort to seize the mad inventor. Frank edged a little closer toward Vilnoff, at the same time trying to hold the maniac in conversation.

"The levers are all set, you say?"

"Ach yes, all set!" chuckled Vilnoff. "De connections have been made. No one can communicate with de outside vorld. Dere is no hope for any of us now. I shall die wid de rest."

Frank had edged a little closer, when he noticed that the man's hands had relaxed on the levers. Joe saw his brother's intention, but realized the space between the lad and Vilnoff was dangerously wide. He had an idea.

"Vilnoff!" Joe shouted in a deep voice.

The inventor swung around, alarmed. He was momentarily deceived by the trick, and that period of hesitancy gave Frank the extra time he needed. He sprang across the open space, flung himself against the man, and

hurled him away from the deadly levers. Vilnoff, however, slipped out of the boy's grasp
like an eel.

"You shall never take me alive!" he
shrieked. "I vould radder die."

Twisting about, he suddenly plunged into a
tiny closet close to an instrument panel on the
wall, and slammed the door behind himself.

"He's escaped!" shouted Joe.

The words were scarcely out of his mouth before there came a livid blue flash that seemed
to leap from the closet door. Then it fell open,
and the limp body of Vilnoff tumbled out,
sprawling on the concrete floor.

"The end of a warped but brilliant brain,"
said Frank as the boys looked down at the
huddled figure soberly. "Perhaps he had that
wire rigged up for just this kind of an emergency."

"Maybe there's a chance yet to save Bayport!" exclaimed Joe.

Frank looked quickly at the electric clock on
the wall.

"Joe, it's midnight! Dad and the police
will be at the west gate! They must be
warned! You'll have to do it, Joe."

"Warn them?" exclaimed his brother. "I
couldn't get there in twenty minutes if I should
run every step of the way. We're a long distance from that gate."

"*Topnotch!* Get the horse and make him race as he has never raced before!"

"But what of you?" quavered Joe.

"I took notes of things around here and maybe I can save the situation yet by crippling the machinery."

"You'll be killed!"

"I'll take that chance," said Frank with set jaws. "But if Vilnoff was telling the truth, this whole place will be destroyed, and Bayport badly damaged. We can't both run away from here and leave all this machinery set as it is. Hurry, Joe. If I come out of this alive I'll go back to the *Sleuth* and return home by water."

No one knew better than did Frank that the odds were strongly against him. Would he be able to foil the dead inventor's diabolical schemes before the twenty and ten minute periods should be up? Every second was precious to him. He grabbed Joe's hand.

"So long, Joe! Do the very best you can."

"Oh gee, Frank, I can't let you do this." Joe's voice was shaky.

"I must," said Frank. "And you must go!"

The Hardy boys knew they might never see each other alive again. Yet there was no use to delay. There was work to be done. Joe turned and went over to the door.

"If I can get above ground," he said, "I'll be off!"

He pressed a pushbutton in the wall. As he suspected, the switch controlled the door mechanism, which swung open before him. He hastened into the next chamber.

From room to room he went, doors opening before him in response to the controlling switches. At last Frank heard him climbing steps.

"I've found a way out," Joe shouted.

Meanwhile Frank was getting busy. He sprang toward the battery of levers. With his heart in his mouth he pulled one back, not knowing if his act would create a tremendous explosion. Nothing happened, however.

Relieved, he threw lever after lever out of position. Only one of them refused to respond. This jammed, and all his efforts to bring it in line with the others were useless. He could not afford to spend any more time struggling with it, so he ran out of the room and into the signal compartment.

There he hastily set every signal working.

Frank then rushed to the switchboard which controlled phones on the grounds, clapped the head-piece to his ears, and plugged in the first number on the apparatus.

"What is it, Chief?" answered a strange voice.

"All clear out!" snapped Frank. "Tell everyone you see."

"Why, what's wrong——?"

"Those are my orders. Leave the place at once."

Frank plugged in another number. A second voice answered respectfully:

"Yes, sir?"

"Warn everyone to clear out immediately and ask no questions. Everything is going to be blown sky-high in less than a quarter of an hour."

He heard a gasp at the other end of the line, then cut the connection short to plug in another call. To the man who answered he gave the same curt message. He kept this up until he had warned everyone to whom he spoke.

Frank was working against time. Now he ran to the chamber that stored the electrical equipment, and snatched up a pair of rubber gloves and a set of pliers.

A switch on the wall which he guessed to be the master switch had caught his eye, so he threw this into reverse. There were others labeled "DYNAMITE CHAMBER," "GUN-POWDER," "HIGH EXPLOSIVE SHELLS," and so on. To make sure of complete destruction of Vilnoff's system he attacked all the wires leading from them. In a frenzy he snipped them with the pliers, and ripped them clear of the wall.

He realized that at any moment he might accidentally set off a connection that would blow him up and lay waste the entire countryside. Yet he worked grimly, hoping to save the lives of innocent people. Frank's aim was to wreck Vilnoff's entire deadly mechanism as completely and as thoroughly as he possibly could.

In the meantime, what had happened to Joe?

When he had clambered through an open trap-door into the night air he did not think that there was one chance in a thousand that he would be able to locate the cabin where *Topnotch* was hidden.

Great was his relief when he stumbled out and found himself on a road not far from the bridge which held the sinister sign post.

Joe ran down the road. As he did so, he was startled by an alarm bell which began to clang behind him. At the same time red lights flashed among the trees, and the hand grew crimson again. Its uncanny fingers twisted convulsively as they had done when the boys had defied its warning.

Not knowing that his brother's activities in the signal control room were already having their effect, the first thought of Joe was that something had gone wrong; that Vilnoff had revived and overcome Frank, and was now signalling for help. For a moment he was almost tempted to go back but decided that it would be better to follow out his original plan.

"Nothing could have happened," he convinced himself finally. "Vilnoff is dead."

He hastened across the bridge and up the road beyond. The distance seemed long, but in reality it was not far to the clearing. Frank and Joe had lost much time following the stream and blundering through the brush. The path cut straight through the thickets, and past the cabin where Ivan was imprisoned.

As he reached this building, the door opened and a figure came running out into the night. The moon appeared from behind a cloud just then, and by its wan radiance Joe recognized Ivan, the jockey.

"Ivan!" Joe shouted, rushing across the clearing. "Ivan!"

The jockey hurried toward him.

"Who is it?" he asked. "Oh, Joe Hardy. I got the note. I've been expecting you. But what happened? The man who was guarding me cleared out a few minutes ago, looking as if he was scared to death. There's a phone in the cabin and he got a message. What's up?"

"Plenty," gasped Joe. "Quick! I know where *Topnotch* is hidden. We must get word out to my father and the police at the west gate. There's a plot—to blow up this whole place—and damage Bayport, too——"

In a few words he told of the proposed twenty, and then ten minute periods of explo-

sions. Ivan was mystified, but asked no further questions. He hurried along at Joe's
side.

The road continued across the clearing and
wound through another stretch of shrubbery
until the next open space unfolded before them.
In the moonlight Joe could see the stable where
Topnotch was hidden.

As he ran toward the building, a new plan
formulated itself in his mind. Joe was not a
skilled horseman and he doubted his ability to
reach the west gate in time, even on *Topnotch.*
Perhaps Ivan might make it!

Moreover, there was another angle to the
affair. The fleeing helpers of Vilnoff should
escape death, of course, but they should not
escape punishment for their secret work. He
would try to have them captured!

Joe stumbled up to the cabin entrance and
tugged at the cross-bar. It fell away and the
door swung open. There was a whinny of welcome from the dark interior of the stable.

"Topnotch!" shouted Ivan gleefully as he
sprang inside.

He returned in a moment leading the high-
spirited animal by the bridle. *Topnotch*
nuzzled his master lovingly.

"Will you ride him?" asked Joe. "Will you
ride him to the west gate?"

Ivan shook his head.

"I won't go without my father," he answered.

"Your father?" exclaimed Joe in surprise.
"Who is he? Is he here?"

"His name is Vilnoff," answered the jockey.

Joe was stunned. Vilnoff the father of Ivan
Evans, the jockey! He could not believe it.

"But your name is Evans."

Ivan shook his head.

"My real name is Vilnoff," he said. "It's a
long story, Joe. My father kidnaped me and
brought me here because he didn't want me to
continue my career as a jockey. I've forgiven
him for it. I won't leave here without him."

Joe laid a hand on the jockey's arm.

"Ivan," he said quietly, "I wish I had
known about this. Your father is dead. He
preferred death to capture, and it is no doubt
best. But you can help to keep innocent people
from dying. Will you ride to the west gate
now and warn *my* father? Look—here's a
map."

Joe whipped out the sketch Frank had found.
On it he pointed to the road leading to the
west gate.

"My father is dead!" said Ivan dully. "You
are sure of that?"

"I'm sorry, Ivan, but it's true."

The jockey nodded. Then, with a muffled
sob, he sprang up onto the horse's back. He

took a quick glance at the note, crouched low, dug his knees into *Topnotch's* sides, and the gallant animal leaped forward as if it were at the raising of a race-track barrier. In a moment horse and rider had vanished into the darkness of the road at the other side of the clearing.

Joe wheeled about and began running toward Road One, which would bring him to the river. He had gone no more than a few steps when the ground suddenly shook violently beneath him, a great tree crashed nearby, and there was a dull, rumbling sound like thunder beneath the earth's surface!

The twenty minutes were up!

CHAPTER XXV

MYSTERIES SOLVED

THE echoes of the explosion died away. Then all was still.

Would there be another one? Had Frank failed? Had he perhaps been killed, trapped there in the underground hideout? These terrifying questions flashed across Joe's mind as he broke into a run and hurried down the road.

At length he came to the gate over which he and Frank had climbed when they had come into the forbidden territory with its electrically charged fence. He vaulted it and hurried on through the night.

Soon the road turned and dipped toward the river. He ran down the slope and at last caught sight of the water gleaming in the moonlight. He stumbled the last remaining paces to the river's edge.

The *Sleuth* was still safe at her anchorage in the inlet. There was now another craft in the bay as well—a bulky, unwieldy barge. A thick hawser tied around a convenient tree-trunk prevented the huge craft from drifting away with the current.

Now that Joe had reached the river in safety and was only a few yards away from the *Sleuth*, he was undecided as to what to do next. Should he wait, on the chance that Frank would eventually find his way to the inlet? Or should he race to Bayport in the boat and notify the police of what had happened?

There had been no more explosions, which was a good sign, he reflected. One ten-minute period had gone by. Frank must have succeeded! He did not know, of course, that the one blast that had occurred had been caused by the jammed lever in the underground control room, and that it had done comparatively little damage.

Joe decided to wait a few minutes. It was just as well that he did so, for soon he heard a confused shouting, followed by a thudding of footsteps on the road above. He slipped into the dark shadow of a clump of trees. In a few moments about a dozen men came running down to the water's edge. They were badly frightened, gabbling among themselves in a foreign language. These were no doubt some of Vilnoff's hirelings, thrown into panic by the working of their master's diabolical scheme.

Joe rushed out of the gloom, and pointed to

the big, flat-bottomed boat. He could see that
the men were panic-stricken and did not know
what to do.

"Take to the barge!" he shouted. "To the
barge!"

They were too frightened to question his au-
thority. One of them with a shout went splash-
ing out into the water and began climbing over
the side of the barge. The others followed
him like so many sheep, knocking one another
down, and fighting for places on the boat.

In the meantime Joe was busy untying the
heavy hawser from the tree trunk. When the
last of the aliens had climbed aboard the boy
hurled the big rope into the water, and cast
the barge adrift.

The current took the craft in its grip and
drew it away from shore. It was some time,
however, before the bewildered foreigners discovered their plight and realized that they were
drifting steadily and remorselessly out into
midstream. When they did, they set up a wild
uproar, screaming imprecations and curses.
But the water was deep and cold. Even if any
of the men were able to swim it was soon evident that none of them intended to risk a
plunge.

"That will hold you fellows for a while," remarked Joe with satisfaction.

He sat down on the bank and watched the

big barge with its terrified freight drift out upon the current that would carry it down the river and into Barmet Bay.

Two more ten-minute periods passed. No further explosions occurred.

A little later Joe heard more voices and footsteps on the road above him.

"How many of Vilnoff's men are there?" muttered Joe, hiding himself again.

Then he heard Frank's voice say, "I told Joe I would come back to the *Sleuth* if I were to get out alive. If he sent Ivan out to the west gate he must have come down here himself."

"What's all the racket out on the river?" demanded another voice.

There were three men with Frank. Each of them carried a flashlight, and Joe caught the gleam of uniform buttons. He stepped out of his hiding place.

"I knew you'd succeed, Frank!" he said grimly.

"Joe! Then you're safe!"

"Not only safe, but I've captured a boatload of prisoners in the bargain. There must be a dozen of Vilnoff's henchmen yelling like mad out in that barge. I set 'em adrift."

Frank and the policemen crowded around Joe Hardy. When he explained what had happened one of the officers uttered a whoop of joy and began running up the road.

"Just what we wanted!" he cried. "We were afraid the others had made a getaway. I'll radio to Headquarters and they'll send a couple of police boats out to tow that gang into Bayport and lock 'em up."

"You caught some others?" inquired Joe.

"A bunch," said the officer.

"I think they got Gus and Pete," Frank commented.

"Good!" said Joe. "They deserve punishment. Some people stoop pretty low to make easy money."

Frank quickly told Joe everything else that had happened. Ivan had reached the west gate with his message. Fenton Hardy and a squad of policemen had already rushed into Vilnoff's "forbidden territory" only to find that the madman's helpers had scattered. Frank had completed his work effectively and rushed out, meeting the police. He had revealed the hiding places of the munitions, which were immediately placed under a strong guard.

"If you don't mind, boys," one of the constables now said to the Hardys, "I'd like to shake hands with you. Seems to me that you fellows saved Bayport from a terrible disaster tonight. When I think of my wife and kiddies asleep at home, not knowin' what threatened 'em——"

He said no more, but extended a rough hand,

which Frank and Joe shook warmly. The other officer did likewise.

"Will we wait here for Dad and Ivan?" asked Joe.

"They're going home by car. We'll meet them at the house."

"Let's go, then."

Before the Hardy boys departed they showed the constable the place where Frank had dumped the case of munitions into the water from the sinister speed-boat.

"Ah! That's good," declared the officer. "The maker's name will be on that box. We'll be able to trace where those things have been coming from."

There was a joyous reunion at the Hardy home in the early hours of that morning when Frank and Joe returned and found their father and Ivan awaiting them. When reports began to pile in from Police Headquarters, after Vilnoff's hirelings had been captured and brought in for questioning, many details of the great munitions plot were exposed.

The munitions had been secretly manufactured at the factory that had exploded on the fateful morning when the Hardy family had discussed mysteries at the breakfast table. The sunken case in the river proved beyond a doubt that it was the origin of the supplies of explosives, and its owners were apprehended.

Vilnoff, as wealthy as he was insane, had been the master-mind of the whole scheme.

"After all," said Ivan, "he was my father and I can't condemn him too harshly. He should have been in an asylum. My mother, you see, was a member of the old Evans family of Bayport. After she married my father they lived abroad until I was about ten years old. Then they came back to America on a visit with the intention of putting me in school here. There was a fire in a hotel in Bayport and my mother—died."

The others listened to Ivan's story in sympathetic silence.

"She died in an attempt to save a man who lived on the same floor of the hotel. He was a politician who had always acted with great bitterness toward my father's country. After my mother's death, my father's mind seemed to become affected. He lived abroad for a while but finally came back to Bayport, when the politician began talking in Washington against my father's country. I can see now that he must have had this terrible scheme brewing in the back of his brain. He was very proud of his delicate hands, and used to make little models of them——"

"Like the hand I found in the garden!"

"And like the one on the sinister sign post, I suppose," admitted Ivan.

"But how about the stealing of *Topnotch?*" asked Fenton Hardy. "What was the reason for that?"

"I ran away from home and became a jockey," said Ivan. "My father was always greatly opposed to that and did everything in his power to stop me. But I loved riding and wouldn't give up my career. So that was why he had *Topnotch* kidnaped—not for the sake of any ransom, but to discourage me from racing any more."

"But a ransom was collected," Frank pointed out.

"The Negro driver whom they found in one of the cabins tonight says that my father never ordered the ransom. He insists the men who stole the horse did that and then didn't dare return *Topnotch* without orders from my father."

"And your own kidnaping?" asked Fenton Hardy.

"I can forgive him that," said Ivan. "Of course, I was never aware of any of his schemes, but when he had me taken to the cabin I knew he had done it simply as a last resort to make me quit the racing game."

"How about Vilnoff's double—the man we saw in the motorboat, the one who sailed for Europe?" inquired Joe.

"My father's brother, I imagine. He had a

twin, an exiled revolutionary from his own country. I think perhaps my uncle had a lot to do with influencing my father."

"We'll probably never see the other Mr. Vilnoff," said Fenton Hardy. "He's safe in hiding on the other side of the water now, I'll be bound."

So the two great mysteries were finally cleared up through the efforts of the Hardy boys. Bayport was saved from great damage and *Topnotch* was returned to his grateful owner, who subsequently insisted on rewarding the boys handsomely for their work. The ransom money was all recovered.

Aunt Gertrude did not hear the story of the night's doings until she came down to breakfast next morning. When she learned that the Hardy home might have been blown off the map during the night she had a sudden attack of faintness.

"Well," she said finally when she was feeling a little better, "I suppose I must admit that you have been brave boys."

Later she was to admit this again after the mystery, "A Figure in Hiding." Right now she felt the Hardy family had been disgraced.

"It will all come out now, that you have been interested in horse-racing. That's how it started, by going to the horse-races. You can't get away from that fact."

"Oh, now, Aunty," pleaded Frank, "horse-racing isn't so bad."

"Anything connected with horses is bad!" snorted Aunt Gertrude. "Never, never would I have anything to do with horses or horse-racing in any shape, manner or form. So there!"

She dug her spoon into a boiled egg so viciously to emphasize her remarks that the top of it jumped halfway across the table. As the boys snickered at this, there was a ring at the doorbell. Frank jumped up.

"I'll answer it," he said.

He returned in a moment with a letter in his hand.

"Special delivery for you, Aunt Gertrude!" he announced.

His relative put on her spectacles and read the missive. An expression of dismay and consternation passed over her face.

"My smelling salts!" she gasped. "Quick!"

Joe rushed forward with them. Aunt Gertrude took a deep whiff and then waved her hand toward the letter.

"Read it!" she said faintly.

Joe did so.

"Miss Gertrude Hardy: As the lawyer entrusted with disposing of the estate of your distant relative, Jonathan Hood, who died in Kentucky two months ago and willed some of

his property to you, may I say that the estate
is largely encumbered with debts.   However,
you will be glad to know that he left you his
only asset—a stable of race-horses!''

"Hurray!'' yelled the Hardy boys, doubling
up with laughter.

THE END